A TEST OF FIRE

A PRIDE AND PREJUDICE VARIATION NOVEL

ELIZABETH ANN WEST

ELIZABETHANNWEST.COM

Email writer@elizabethannwest.com

Paperback ISBN: 978-1-944345-28-0

Ebook ISBN: 978-1-944345-26-6

When two new eligible bachelors move into the neighborhood, the Meryton Assembly becomes a more exciting harvest celebration than ever before. Couples dance and make new acquaintances, reveling in so many possibilities the evening presents . . . until the shout of "FIRE!" echoes from overhead.

Scrambling for safety separates Elizabeth Bennet from her sister, Jane. Frightened that she might lose the person she loves best in all the world, Lizzy sets aside her fear and rushes back in to the burning building. Overwhelmed by the heat and falling debris, suddenly it's Elizabeth in desperate need of saving!

When the burned out shell of the tavern and assembly rooms are left smoldering in the early morning hours, many families have lost too much. The Bennet family sits vigil over the injured Lizzy, praying that she wakes up. They are joined by another, the very man who carried her out in his arms: Mr. Darcy.

Enjoy this twist of Jane Austen's original *Pride and Prejudice* that imagines how a fire at the Meryton Assembly might have changed the story. Join over 30,000 readers who have followed the story on Fanfiction.net since October 1, 2021 when author Elizabeth Ann West offered five story prompts to her reader group and they selected one for her to write as quickly as possible for them. They also picked out the "Easter eggs" you can find in the Acknowledgements section.

A Test of Fire is a feel-good path of healing and overcoming survivor's guilt for Our Dear Couple. You don't want to miss it!

❀ Created with Vellum

Thank you to my author friend, Chris Cox, for asking me constantly if my words were done. For April Floyd, always being just a phone call away, when a girl needs help. And a huge thank you to my sister, Christine Schilling, for joining on making all the big moves!

FOREWORD

The story before your eyes is a return for me back to ways I wrote the first three years I was writing Jane Austen Fan Fiction. Before the divorce. Before I lost 200 pounds of dead weight . . . his name was Josh.

Single and settled, I have so many story outlines itching to have their days of writing. This story elbowed all of them out of the way . . . sort of. At the end of September 2021 I was working through strengths training offered by Becca Syme, based on the Clifton StrengthsFinder test.

For those who take the test, I am Strategic, Activator, Ideation, Focus, Self-Assurance. The

StrengthsFinder isn't a magic bullet; to me it was permission to stop trying to be someone I'm not.

But now, 3 years from when I first started to aggressively pursue healing from my divorce, it's about optimizing who I am. I can't lie to myself, which means if my brain *knows* under ideal circumstances I could dictate and write X chapters or words before a deadline for a book (a preorder deadline in the past), I would not write. I would sit and wait until the very last possible moment to write and then . . . inevitably something derailing would come along and I'd miss the deadline.

Many of you have seen me not make preorder deadlines in the past. That's why I don't use that tool, anymore. Instead, I will only use it in the future if the book is completely written and done. But who wants to WAIT after a book is done until they can have it? No one. I know I don't as a reader.

What does this mean for my writing?

A Test of Fire was my test to see what would happen if instead of deadlines, I went back to "fast as I can?" Turns out, right now, fast as I can produces a novel in 6 weeks.

I think we can work with that. :)

If you would like to be a part of shaping future stories I write in challenge mode, join the Facebook group #TheJaneside. I also offer readers a chance to submit "Easter eggs," a list for this book you'll find in Acknowledgements, along with all of the screen names of readers who left reviews as I was writing this book.

Thank you, everyone, for this journey and opportunity to share my stories with you. I know it's been a rough couple of years for all of us. But like the meme running around right now says: we're all going to walk quietly into 2022. No one declare it your year, don't touch anything, and don't make any loud noises. :)

We got this!

Elizabeth Ann West

ALSO BY ELIZABETH ANN WEST

The Trouble With Horses

Very Merry Mischief

To Capture Mr. Darcy

The Whisky Wedding

If Mr. Darcy Dared (mature)

Mr. Darcy's Twelfth Night (mature)

THE MORALITIES OF MARRIAGE SERIES

By Consequence of Marriage

A Virtue of Marriage

The Blessing of Marriage

The Trappings of Marriage

The Miracle of Marriage

The Fruits of Marriage (TBA)

THE SEASONS OF SERENDIPITY SERIES

A Winter Wrong

A Spring Sentiment

A Summer Shame

An Autumn Accord

A Winter Wonder

A January for Jane (bonus novella)

From Longbourn to Pemberley (Boxed Set, Year One)

A Spring Society

A May for Mary

Shop all of Elizabeth's books by visiting her site:

www.elizabethannwest.com

CHAPTER 1

The Assembly Rooms in Meryton pulsed with joyous celebration for the end of the harvest season. Nearly every family in the surrounding hamlets of Meryton, Netherfield, and Longbourn were represented. The air inside became thick and cloying, a mixture of honeyed wine and butterscotch from the ground floor warred with the scents of wax candles and tobacco smoke from the upstairs card tables.

Years of struggle fell from memory as many farms enjoyed the most bountiful harvests. The dancing, revelry, and card games began promptly at eight o'clock in the evening. Elizabeth Bennet, the second eldest daughter of the Bennet family of Longbourn, stared most curiously over at the party accompanying the newest resident of Netherfield Park, a Mr. Charles Bingley.

The gentleman, Mr. Bingley, she assessed to be jovial and kind. The man secured sets with her elder sister Jane, and also her friend Charlotte Lucas. Elizabeth respected that Mr. Bingley, as the newest bachelor in the area, solicited dances with the eldest daughters of each prominent family. He was first standing up with Mrs. Long's niece, Harriet.

Mr. Bingley's sisters were another matter altogether. Their costumes stood out in fashion and form compared to the other ladies in the room. A local assembly such as Meryton would never rival the ballrooms of London for adherence to the latest fashion plates. With the youngest in a bright, shimmery tangerine and the elder, married sister in a deep amethyst gown, each laughed and mocked the frocks around them skillfully behind fluttering fans.

The two Bingley sisters remained noticeably close to the other gentleman that had arrived with them, a Mr. Darcy of Derbyshire. After Mr. Darcy asked Miss Bingley to a set, Elizabeth passed by Mr. Bingley's eldest sister, Mrs. Hurst, to overhear a harsh criticism spoken to her husband.

"What a tragic waist on that one, there, dancing with Charles. Her family must not have any means to dress her properly," Mrs. Hurst sneered as her portly husband nodded in agreement.

Elizabeth disliked those two immediately, even though Harriet Long was not one of her favorite confidants in the surrounding area, no one deserved derision by utter strangers. She moved away from the complaining woman for the duration of the set and watched the spinning couples from the vantage point of the punch bowl.

"Do you see those two gentlemen?" Mrs. Bennet, the mother of five daughters, asked her husband Mr. Bennet, who politely nodded and smiled at the lady to his right, but did not otherwise concern himself with Mrs. Bennet's question. "Mr. Bingley seems very amiable. He could be a perfect match for one of our girls."

"Mmmm," the bookish man intoned. "The younger of them is not so bad... but the elder. Oh my, what a fright. With that dark coat and pale face, I should think he is a ghost risen from the dead." Mr. Bennet could not resist a smile as he sipped from a crystal glass of Madeira. "I should hope not him, for he appears to be a frightfully bad dancer."

Mr. Bennet, who was a keen observer of society's foibles and frivolities, appeared to his wife to show great attention to her prattle. He caught his daughter Elizabeth's eye and winked as she walked past her parents.

If she had given them the same judgment as she had the Hursts, she would find their behavior just as appalling. Instead, the unfamiliarity of the stranger failed to redeem the Hursts while expecting her parents' behavior made her overlook their trespasses.

Having to sit out sets due to a shortage of gentlemen, Elizabeth made it her new mission to learn more about Mr. Darcy, who she noticed spoke to no one outside of his party. His behavior tempted her curiosity. As she neared his person, Mr. Bingley approached him, encouraging him to dance again. Elizabeth smiled as she heartily agreed with Mr. Bingley finding fault with his friend when there was such a shortage of partners in the room. What she did not expect was Mr. Bingley incorporating her proximity into his plans of scolding.

"Come, Darcy," said he,"I must have you dance. I hate to see you standing about by yourself in this stupid manner. You had much better dance."

Elizabeth found herself nodding with Mr. Bingley's good sense.

"I certainly shall not. You know how I detest it, unless I am particularly acquainted with my partner. It's such an assembly as this, it would be insupportable. Your sisters are engaged for the next set, and there is not another woman in the room, whom it would not be a punishment to me to stand up with."

Elizabeth caught herself in mid-squawk at the man's rudeness. His behavior matched so closely to Mr. Bingley's elder sister! She had hoped Mr. Darcy was merely shy, not prejudiced against those of lesser means. Instead, her highest hopes for the man shattered from his utter disdain for every lady in the room.

"I would not be so fastidious as you are," cried Bingley, "for a kingdom! Upon my honor, I never met with so many pleasant girls in my life, as I have this evening; and there are several of them you see uncommonly pretty."

Elizabeth giggled at Mr. Bingley's assessment, catching the eye of her friend Charlotte Lucas across the way. Charlotte silently shook her head with a look of disapproval. She knew quite well what consequences could arise from her friend's game of spying on others.

"*You* are dancing with the only handsome girl in the room," said Mr. Darcy, looking at the eldest Miss Bennet.

"Oh! She is the most beautiful creature I ever beheld! But there is one of her sisters sitting down just behind you, who is very pretty, and I dare say very agreeable. Do let me ask my partner to introduce you."

"Which do you mean?" Turning round, Mr. Darcy looked for a moment at Elizabeth, catching her eye.

Elizabeth found herself short of breath and utterly captivated by the twisted look of pain on the man's face. Her sense of empathy disappeared as he withdrew his gaze and coldly said, "She is tolerable; but not handsome enough to tempt *me*; and I am in no humor at present to give consequence to young ladies who are slighted by other men. You had better return to your partner and enjoy her smiles, for you are wasting your time with me."

Mr. Bingley shook off his friend's negative attitude to rejoin the festivities and Elizabeth narrowed her eyes at the back of the man who had so thoroughly insulted her that she wished to thrash him. Her memories of cruel boys in her childhood and their wicked taunts led her straight to the safety of Charlotte Lucas and her brother, John. John had been one of those young lads that earned himself more than one injury at Elizabeth's hands, growing up in the rustic countryside before they were all expected to join polite society. Thankfully, he had improved with age where it appeared Mr. Darcy had not.

"You shall never believe what Mr. Darcy just said, directly in front of me. Apparently, I am tolerable, but not handsome enough to tempt him to dance with me," she recounted with a brief embrace of her friend as a greeting, then crossing her arms in ire.

"Lizzy, serves you right for eavesdropping," Charlotte admonished, but John laughed.

"Dueling pistols at dawn then? Clearly, his eyesight is not good. Though alternatively, we could have Father command that he dance with you," John said, looking around for his father who relished his role as Master of Ceremonies at every assembly.

"Dueling . . . commandments?" Charlotte asked, mishearing her brother by only catching a few words.

Their group was soon approached by Mr.

Bingley and Elizabeth realized the man was attempting to make amends for his friend, or else he had run out of eldest daughters and moved on to the second born. No matter how kind Mr. Bingley was to her, Elizabeth felt no desire for further attachment to him; that state she happily reserved for her sister Jane who could not stop looking in Mr. Bingley's direction all evening long.

"Aye, Charlotte, we shall write ten," Elizabeth said, confusing her friend even further, but earning a laugh from John.

"Miss Elizabeth, may I have the honor of this dance?" Mr. Bingley asked and Elizabeth accepted.

During the dance, Mr. Bingley did indeed apologize for his friend's behavior but Lizzy laughed it off.

"He did say that he detested dancing," she said as she moved with the steps to meet Mr. Bingley in the middle, and then return back to the line. "I can hardly hold the opinion of a man so defective in his social graces to high esteem."

"Defective, oh, in his social graces, oh, I see, well done!" Mr. Bingley said, enjoying Miss Elizabeth's sharp wit against his friend. He was much more accustomed to the universal deference and simpering his wealthy friend enjoyed wherever he went than stern rejection.

Elizabeth smiled at the man in question as he watched her dance with Mr. Bingley most intently. Given the friendship between the two men, she suspected her words would reach him by his friend's recounting after the conclusion of the dance. And that assumption is what began her second game of the evening: to stay as far away as possible from Mr. Darcy for the duration.

This new game proved trickier than the last, for her sister Jane and Mr. Bingley soon found ways to speak in every interval between dances, and Mr. Darcy stood often near his friend. This prompted Elizabeth to constantly walk away from the party until she ran directly into John Lucas again.

"Shall I state you are handsome enough to tempt me, Lizzy? Shall we dance?" John Lucas teased his sister's friend and Elizabeth laughed at the sentiment. She had long passed over any superficial desires for John Lucas back when he went away to school in London at fifteen, mostly because he returned with no marked improvement in his thoughts despite the training.

"Yes, we shall, but you need not flatter my vanity."

"It is the Boulanger, perhaps we'll find you a husband, yet," John Lucas responded.

Unfortunately, they found themselves in a grouping with none other than Jane, Mr. Bingley, Mrs. Hurst, and her dance partner, Mr. Darcy, and Elizabeth's remaining sisters with their partners. The exact grouping she had hoped to avoid until she spied a telling grin from John Lucas, she realized he had led her directly to the group of her sisters on purpose! Elizabeth scowled as Mr. Darcy seemingly aided in the setup when he grasped her other hand and she was forced to skip and make merry dancing around a circle between the two men.

She stood stoically next to the offending man as Mr. Lucas happily took his circuits with half of the ladies in the ring. A pit in her stomach began to form as she counted ahead and realized due to the formation, she would have to twirl and spin with Mr. Darcy no less than two times per cycle and she resolved to not meet his eye. Of course, this mettle became tested the very first time they took a spin as he grasped her hands with gentle firmness, stronger than the other men, and she looked up in surprise. His dark brown eyes remained in pain and once again, her sympathy for the man came from a deep place in her heart, overruling her mind's indignance over his existence.

"I hope I'm performing *tolerably*," she called out as they had rejoined the circle and she followed behind him, knowing her words would reach him as she faced his direction.

The circle changed directions and she now had her back to Mr. Darcy, following behind John Lucas, holding hands with both men.

"Indeed, I am tempted," Mr. Darcy stated.

Elizabeth caught her breath and blushed as she had to stand next to him again, appearing unaffected while Mr. Lucas took his spins with Jane and her younger sister, Kitty.

A shriek above and abrupt screeching of the violin paralyzed the dancing groups below as thick, black smoke began to fill the ceiling from the balcony. The adults playing cards above where they could safely look down and chaperone their charges were in an uproar, jostling the musicians in the balcony who all stood, holding their instruments as though prepared to do battle.

"Fire!" yelled a voice above stairs, and Elizabeth felt time slow to a stop.

At first, no one moved a muscle in response, until everyone attempted to move at once!

"No!" she screamed, her eyes glued to the

sight while her heart beat so fast she could feel it in her bones. Every person on the dance floor jostled for the sides of the room, heading towards the doors. People thundered down the stairs. Couples grabbed one another holding on despite the rush.

John Lucas abandoned Elizabeth to search for his sisters, and behind her, a loud crash heralded the subsequent sound of shattering glass. Someone had thrown a chair at the wide, sashed windows in the front. More men picked up chairs to smash the windows, a deafening clatter until a few gave way.

The sudden gush of air fed the flames and more screams upstairs pierced the din. Elizabeth felt herself carried out the front door in the sea of people. She gagged on smoke feeling in her heart something was terribly wrong. Within moments she stood outside with three of her sisters: Lydia, Kitty, and Mary.

But there was no Jane.

"Jane!" Elizabeth screamed as she coughed from inhaling the smoke. "Jane?" She searched all of the groupings of people around her as some of the men and women ran away, and others called for buckets to begin a brigade. Others had gone to the barn to bring out the horses and livestock as the fire appeared to have begun in the tavern next door. Everywhere Elizabeth looked there was chaos, but she could not find her sister who should have been right behind her.

Elizabeth abandoned her younger sisters to rush back to the front door, but people continued to spill out, though fewer in number.

"Stop, Elizabeth!" A pair of strong hands grasped her shoulder, shocking her by using only her first name. She spun around to see Mr. Darcy keeping her from entering the building once more.

"But I must, my sister!" she screamed, stomping hard on the man's foot to escape his grasp, she climbed back in through a smashed window, caring not that her gloved hand now bled freely from the cut glass.

Immediately, the thick smoke overtook her and she collapsed to her hands and knees, gasping for air. What little oxygen her lungs found felt too hot to breathe. Crawling along the floor, littered with debris and glass, and now dotted with burning embers from the ceiling above, Elizabeth tried to search for her sister. The heat and lack of visibility proved too strong, and she managed only a few feet, touching the hand of someone on the floor. She willed her eyes to open, despite the stinging temperatures and smoke to see it was not Jane, but Charlotte Lucas.

A burst of pain tormented her feet and Elizabeth kicked out. She mustered all her remaining strength to roll away, trying to pull Charlotte with her. But Charlotte would not budge even a few inches. Elizabeth tried to cry, but her tears were taken by the blazing heat before they could fall.

She was too late.

Realizing she was about to match Charlotte's fate, she let go and continued to roll, covering her face with her bloodied hands, in what she believed to be the direction of the front door.

Just as she resigned herself to death, someone lifted her from the ground as though she weighed nothing at all. Her last thoughts were of angels raising her out of the burning inferno of a Hell that had claimed her friend and possibly her dearest sister.

CHAPTER 2

Elizabeth Bennet fluttered her eyes open. A blurry image appeared, hovering before her like a watery reflection in a puddle. Blinking, Elizabeth willed the blurriness to disappear, but it hung in the blackness, suspended from a dark sky. Slowly, she focused, and her sister Jane came into view. Exhausted by the effort, she closed her eyes once more, sinking into a deep peace from being reunited with her sister.

For a brief moment, she believed they must have perished together. But as she opened her eyes again, searing pain ripped through her body from her feet up through the top of her head. She cried out, but her throat was too dry and the scream came out scratchy, scarcely audible.

"Oh, Lizzy!" Jane exclaimed as Elizabeth's

thrashing knocked the teacup off the small table next to their shared bed.

Thunderous shouts and scrambling from the hall came bursting into their room as their father and three younger sisters came to see the miracle for themselves.

Mr. Bennet's bottom jaw quivered at the sight of his battered child, finally conscious after the fire two nights ago. He rushed to her bedside but hesitated to touch her as her hands were bandaged and her legs had sustained burns from where her gown caught on fire. Dropping to his knees, he bowed his head in prayer.

"Merciful Lord, we are grateful that you have restored to us what we feared lost," he uttered.

Elizabeth tried to swallow, but her mouth was still dry and her hands useless. She looked to Jane and mimed with her cracked, dry lips to signal she wished to have a drink.

"She's thirsty!" Kitty exclaimed, and Jane rushed out of the room to seek more tea. She reached the kitchens where Hill stood with a fresh tray at the ready, prepared at the sound of good news upstairs.

"Is it Miss Lizzy?"

"She's awake!" Jane said, to the cheers of the servants behind Hill, back in the kitchen. She reached out to take the tray, but Hill refused. She insisted she would carry it up behind her. Jane took two steps and then urged Hill to go up without her. Turning around, she walked over to her father's study where the door stood ajar, and inside, a man paced back and forth before the window.

"My sister has awakened," she said.

A pair of distressed brown eyes gave Miss Bennet his full consideration. "Has she spoken?"

Jane shook her head. "She tried to, but the smoke . . . I am certain once she has some tea, perhaps. I'm sorry, Mr. Darcy, I really must go and see to her needs."

"Yes, yes, of course," he said, picking up his hat from the chair he had frequented so often in the last two days.

"If I might be of any service . . ." he began, but Miss Bennet had already left. Suddenly, he felt as though he were intruding and thought it best to return to Netherfield Park and carry the good news to Mr. Bingley, who would undoubtedly wish to bring his good tidings tomorrow when they met for the funeral service for the fallen. Twenty souls lost, but at least it had not been twenty-one.

Taking his hat in his hand, he felt quite dumb

that he had not thought to summon his physician! But that was one circumstance he could remedy. Alone in Mr. Bennet's study, he pulled out parchment and a quill and began to write his missive.

Above stairs, Jane poked her head into her mother's room, but Mrs. Bennet remained abed, keeping the room dark.

"Jane?" croaked out Mrs. Bennet before the eldest Bennet daughter could rejoin the sister who had risked her life for her safety. Of course, Lizzy would have died in that search if not for Mr.Darcy; Jane had escaped through the back door when the panic spread throughout the assembly room.

"Yes, Mama. Lizzy has awakened."

"Praises to the Lord and His highest angels you were spared the loss of a dear sister," Mrs. Bennet said, weeping. Aunt Phillips had been playing cards upstairs at the assembly and sitting closest to where the fire broke out. She had not managed to escape. How the blaze occurred, no one fully understood, but the origin paled in priority compared to the outcome.

Jane grimaced as she wanted her mother to rejoice that one of her offspring was spared. But she held her tongue from any criticism. Lizzy was not healed yet and Jane felt unsure of even considering her own devastation if Elizabeth had not awakened.

"I shall see to Lizzy," she said, as though her mother had worried about who would see to her daughter's care.

Back in the room, Mary spooned small amounts of tea to Elizabeth's fragile lips. Mr. Bennet paced in an agitated state, frustrated by his inability to ease the pain of his favorite.

"You cannot move, Child! Your legs were badly scorched and Mr. Jones worried you might not recover. The bandages . . ." he began, looking around the room for the basin. Finding the bowl with fresh bandages in the water, he tested the temperature to find the water had gone warm. "Hill!" he cried, and the housekeeper suddenly appeared. "Cold water, the coldest from the pump," he demanded.

"Father, she is in pain. She cannot help but writhe," Jane soothed, stepping forward with the bottle that was usually trusted only to the lady of the house. With her mother out of commission in her grief, it became Jane's burden to administer the laudanum. She placed a drop in the next spoonful Mary was about to dribble into Elizabeth's mouth. "This will help you rest, and when you wake again, we can talk to you more and learn if there are any injuries we have missed," Jane said, calmly, taking over the tea duties from Mary.

Kitty and Lydia stood in the back of the room, still frightened to get too close to Lizzy.

When the fresh bowl of cold water arrived, Jane sighed as Elizabeth was now beginning to slumber lightly.

"Father, you have slept not a wink. Why don't you find some rest and I will change Lizzy's bandages."

"Jane, you take too much upon yourself," the man replied with gratitude, suddenly aging before her very eyes from his exhaustion finally settling in.

"You girls too, I will need Mary and Kitty to sit with Lizzy tonight."

"What about Lydia?" Kitty asked, making Jane smile. Despite the calamity before them, her sisters could still find cause to squabble. The small glimmer of normal life before the fire gave her the oddest sense of hope.

"Lydia can stay with me and read for Lizzy. Can't you, Lyddie?" Jane asked, and the youngest Bennet sister nodded assent, even though reading aloud was her least favorite thing to do.

Soon the room emptied and Jane was left with nothing but the unpalatable task of tending to her sister's wounds. The cuts and minor burns on her hands would heal the fastest, Mr. Jones predicted. And if there was scarring, it would be along her palm, unnoticeable. Jane also felt her sister would mind less the injuries to her hands because so often they wore gloves outside of close family and friends. The real problem was her legs.

Gently, Jane shifted the coverlet just to the middle of Elizabeth's shins and watched her sister closely for distress. Lizzy moaned, and Lydia paused in reading the book of Hamlet they had been using to keep their patient company.

"Keep reading, she is well. This is never easy," Jane encouraged Lydia.

Bandages soaked in an odd yellowish coloring with tinges of blood covered both of Elizabeth's legs from the tops of her feet to just a few inches above her ankles. Jane gave another prayer of thanksgiving that the injury was not more extensive up Elizabeth's calves, or worse, to her thighs, which would have been fatal. It wasn't clear how her gown caught on fire, but the assumption was that embers from the ceiling must have fallen onto her skirts as she was searching. That same ceiling collapsed just moments after Mr. Darcy stumbled out with Elizabeth in his arms.

Jane felt a wave of guilt pass over her as she tenderly removed the first bandage. She followed Mr. Jones' instructions and breathed deeply to detect if there was any foul odor coming from the wound. But the oozing, angry pink and red flesh exposed to the air gave none. She held Elizabeth's leg down as she removed the others for washing, as once the first was removed, her sister attempted to avoid further discomfort in her sleep.

When at last the skin was exposed, Jane cringed over the next part. Lifting the bottle of the treatment left by Mr. Jones, a foul-smelling liquid made chiefly of diluted vinegar and urine, Jane beckoned Lydia over to the bedside.

"Please, no," Lydia whispered, refusing to put down the book.

"We must. You know we must," Jane said sweetly as though what they did next was akin to unpleasant lessons in the schoolroom. "Do you want to hold or dab?"

"Dab," Lydia said, putting it upon Jane to move out of the way and prepare to brace all of her weight on Lizzy's thighs.

"Ready?"

Lydia nodded, the mixture in hand, and dipped the sponge into the bowl.

Jane took a deep breath and pressed herself against Elizabeth's strongest muscles and Lydia hesitantly dabbed the injuries.

"Faster!" Jane urged as Elizabeth grew restless.

A new outcome of the searing treatment manifested quickly, the direct result of their care just moments before. Elizabeth Bennet let out a soul-piercing scream. Followed by another, and another.

Lydia froze and Jane began to bark orders.

"Get the bandages!" she grunted and began to blow on Elizabeth's ankles to try to cease her sister's thrashing and howls of misery.

"What?" Lydia asked as the racket was loud.

"Bandages!" Jane yelled.

A story below, Mr. Darcy clenched his knuckles tightly. At first, he was elated to hear the best news that Elizabeth had awoken, but that unearthly screams unsettled him to his core. He warred with the rules and boundaries of polite society. Why was no one helping her?

"Pardon me, sir," Hill said as she hurried up the stairs to the girls' room.

Deciding that he could accept the consequences that came, he braved entering the private sanctuary of the Bennet household, one reserved for the most intimate of family members and not visitors like him. He rushed up the stairs as the screaming continued.

The room Elizabeth was set up in was the second one to the left, and he stood in the doorway to spy utter chaos. The youngest sister stood in the middle, crying and paralyzed with fear. Miss Bennet's hair had fallen from its pins as she tried to explain what needed to be done and keep Elizabeth from further harming herself.

Confidently, Mr. Darcy strode into the room, gently nudged Lydia to the side, and spoke with a calm, baritone voice.

"How may I assist?"

Jane began to speak, but noticed at the sound of Mr. Darcy's voice lessened her sister's thrashing.

"Keep speaking, sir," she whispered, nodding to Hill towards the bandages.

Mr. Darcy looked around the room and spied the abandoned tome of Shakespeare in the chair. Lifting it he began to recite:

To be, or not to be -- that is the question.

Whether 'tis nobler in the mind to suffer

Elizabeth stilled and Jane and Hill made quick work of applying the fresh cool bandages to her tormented skin. Still, Mr. Darcy cleared his throat and continued, his delivery steady and methodical, rivaling the clarity of tone of any London actor.

The slings and arrows of outrageous fortune,
Or to take arms against a sea of troubles
And, by opposing, end them.

Jane sighed in relief and stood next to Mr. Darcy as they watched Elizabeth settle down, back to slumbering, albeit with labored breathing. Jane stepped forward once Hill retreated and replaced the coverlet over Elizabeth's feet, removing the slight indecency to her modesty in front of Mr. Darcy.

"Thank you, Mr. Darcy. My father has been with her night and day, reading to her. She must have thought you were him," Jane explained and it struck her as uncanny that the moment Mr. Darcy spoke, her sister responded.

"Of course. I am happy to have been of what little service I could," he stated, then recalled his letter down in the study. "I am sending for my physician in London."

"That is very kind of you, though I do think she is mending well."

Mrs. Bennet suddenly appeared in the doorway, thankfully wrapped in her robe, though entirely inappropriately dressed for Mr. Darcy's presence.

"Jane? Jane? Oh, Mr. Darcy! Whatever are you doing in here, sir?"

Mr. Darcy's eyes widened in shock at Mrs. Bennet's disarray, and Jane cringed with embarrassment.

"Mr. Darcy helped with Lizzy's care. He read out loud while Hill and I changed her bandages," Jane explained as Lydia suddenly bolted from the room, afraid she might get scolded for being in a room with a gentleman.

"Where is your father?"

Mr. Darcy handed the book to Miss Bennet and bowed to her mother. "I believe he has finally given in to his exhaustion. I am so sorry for your family's loss and realize I am intruding. Forgive me."

He glanced back to take one last look at Elizabeth, though to Mrs. Bennet it appeared Mr. Darcy was looking back at Jane, and then removed himself from the room after Mrs. Bennet moved away from the door.

Stepping into the room her two eldest shared and seeing Elizabeth pale and lying on the bed, she sniffed and made a face of disgust. "He must truly have an interest in you Jane, to come into the sick room."

Jane closed her eyes as her mortification finally registered outside of the crisis. There was nothing pleasant about caring for Elizabeth's needs in her current state, but the man had been ever-present nearly night and day since the tragedy.

"I don't believe it was my benefit he sought out, Mama. Would you like a tray of food?" Jane offered, realizing that her sister would be fine for a short time.

"Yes, yes I believe I should eat," Mrs. Bennet agreed, slowly approaching Elizabeth's sleeping form. She bent down to press a kiss to her daughter's forehead, and then gently patted Elizabeth's matted hair. "You are always so strong, my Lizzy."

Jane gaped at the sudden tenderness from their mother but didn't dare to say a word. When her mother was finished with the maternal ministrations she cared to offer, she smiled weakly at Jane.

"You take so much upon yourself, Janie. Mind that you also care for yourself," she said, leaving the stench of the sickroom behind to return to her own bed.

Jane laid down on the extra bed her father had moved into their shared room from the guest room. It was small and not so tightly strung, so the mattress sank a few inches when she rolled onto it, not bothering to change into a shift.

She stared at her injured sister, sleeping fitfully and observed her wince and grimace in her sleep, but not open her eyes. Even though she realized Elizabeth was still in considerable discomfort, seeing her sister fight and respond to the pain was far preferable to before when they were unsure if she would awaken again.

"If I was in that bed, you'd do the same for me," she said, with a yawn. "Only you'd manage it so much better. They'd all listen to you," she said dreamily, before finally allowing herself to take a rest as well.

CHAPTER 3

Riding his horse, Mr. Darcy hugged the curve along the dirt road leading to Netherfield Park and let the gray go at a trot. His thoughts were consumed with Elizabeth, and he turned over every possible treatment in his mind. Dr. Frederick Stevens, an old friend and healer, would send back word by morning and Mr. Darcy planned to take his carriage to London in the afternoon, after the church service for the fallen.

His thoughts turned to Elizabeth's ghastly face and a wicked feeling of uselessness tugged at his heart. His greatest hope in fetching his physician was to keep Elizabeth alive.

After a groom took control of his horse, he sighed in perfect rhythm to his footsteps up the worn, stone steps of the leased mansion. To his regret, Caroline Bingley stood there ready to greet him.

"I'm so glad you are back, Mr. Darcy. We shall have a pleasant dinner tonight, all in your honor, sir," she offered, batting her eyes at him to elicit a compliment.

"Whatever for?" he asked, immediately regretting encouraging her engagement.

"For your heroism, of course!" she stated, scoffing, but the man held his hands up to discourage her.

"I will take a tray in my room. I need to pack and leave for London tomorrow, but I will return the following day." He used the bannister and changed the direction of his feet, to return to the ground floor. "I ought to speak to your brother."

He managed to walk a half dozen steps across the Italian marble tiles in the foyer, separated by onyx diamond spacers in each corner, before Caroline called after him. She hurried to his side to thwart his progress.

"But why must you leave? We should all quit this dreary country and not return! Since the fire, no one wishes to entertain and be sociable," she said with a pout.

Mr. Darcy battled an intense rage tightening

in his chest. "Entertain and be sociable?" he began, turning away from her to choose his words more carefully. "They've lost . . ."

"Darcy! You're back! Fancy a game of billiards?" Mr. Bingley entered the main foyer from the east side of the house as Darcy had nearly reached the steps. The two friends differed greatly in how they distracted themselves from tragedy.

"No, I don't fancy a game," he spat, and then thought better of insulting his host. "I will, in just a quarter hour," he explained, calculating the time it would take to instruct his man to pack his things.

"I've been waiting for you for over an hour."

"I was delayed."

"Delayed? Doing what?" Bingley asked, most curious about Mr. Darcy's constant disappearances away from Netherfield Park.

Mr. Darcy glanced over at Miss Bingley, wishing he had waited until he was alone with his friend to share his plans. Still, he did not wish to say more than necessary, and so he changed the subject entirely.

"Charles, I must away tomorrow and fetch my physician. But if your hospitality still holds, I should like to return the following day. The day after that at the latest," Darcy added as a last moment addendum. He considered that Dr. Stevens might have affairs to put in order before a protracted stay in Hertfordshire. His mind wandered to accommodating the doctor, unclear if Longbourn would have room, or if the man should stay at Netherfield Park.

"Are you ill? I believed you were not injured in saving Miss Eliza," Miss Bingley suddenly fretted over Mr. Darcy's person, approaching him to see more clearly the invisible injury or malady he had kept hidden.

Darcy waved his hand in the air to encourage her to keep her distance. He had suffered a minor cough from the smoke, but experience with fires had taught him what to do. Before he ran in after Miss Elizabeth he had wet his cravat and covered his mouth.

Never had he felt such a rush as when he found her just by the door, able to save her from certain death. The housekeeper at Longbourn, Hill he believed her name was, had prepared him tea with licorice root and mint, and the slight congestion in his chest cleared up by the next morning.

"No, I am not unwell, the doctor is for the

Bennets. Miss Elizabeth awoke this morning, but she is still gravely injured."

"Was Miss Bennet well?" Mr. Bingley asked, earning a glare from both his sister and his friend. He stammered, and then asked about the others in the household. "And - and, Mrs. Bennet, and the other sisters?"

Darcy sighed, gripping the bannister tightly in his frustrations. "Mrs. Bennet is struggling with the loss of her sister, one of the card players above stairs, but I don't believe I made her acquaintance."

Mr. Bingley shook his head, contradicting his friend. "Her husband is the man who handled the contract for the lease."

Darcy suddenly recollected the connection. "Ah, the woman was very kind when we visited the first time."

"And loud and told us all about her unwed nieces and the entail on the estate," Caroline added, not caring how ill-bred it appeared to speak poorly of the dead. Mr. Darcy had ferried himself back and forth from Longbourn numerous times a day since the fire, and Miss Bingley wished she had thought to feign an injury from it as well. Then, perhaps, his attention would be on her as she had planned at the beginning of the trip.

Mr. Darcy shrugged. "It is still a heavy loss for the family, and if I have any resource in my power to prevent additional loss, I shall dutifully extend it," he said solemnly to the siblings. Bidding them adieu, he finally walked up the stairs in peace.

Caroline took a step as though to follow him, but Mr. Bingley grabbed her arm.

"I thought you were going to visit the Bennets today, like we agreed," he whispered, hoarsely.

"I—I—I—"

"I cannot go by myself and you ought to have visited with Louisa to share your condolences and concern. Then I can visit the next time with you," Mr. Bingley urged.

Caroline stepped away from her brother, looking up the stairs for the man she truly wished to please, and then back to the annoying older brother she abided until either she married or turned five and twenty to control her dowry.

"Mr. Darcy seemed able to visit on his own," she scolded, with an accusatory tone.

"He is different."

"How? Don't say it's his money, Charles, it's vulgar. We have more status than the sonless

Bennets." Caroline began to walk away from the stairs back to her more pleasing activity of strolling up and down in the ballroom on the first floor. There, she imagined one day being mistress of Pemberley and presiding over many of the best families in England at her first ball.

"It's different because he has no designs on any of the daughters. He told me he did not think any of them handsome, except for Jane. And I believe Jane to be the loveliest woman I have ever set my eyes upon . . ." Mr. Bingley explained, with a dreamy expression on his face.

"You think Mr. Darcy likes Jane?" Caroline asked, coming to an abrupt halt. When her brother remained silent, she turned around to look at him, expecting an answer.

Mr. Bingley nodded.

"I don't believe he will rival me, mostly he is fulfilling his Christian duty. But I don't want her to become attached to *him*. I need you to visit, Caro," he said with a plea in his voice. He schooled his expression to one of pure need, not daring to reveal the truth of why he was so desperate to call on Miss Bennet without raising expectations. At least, not until he spoke to her privately.

Caroline Bingley stood still as she considered

her options carefully. On one hand, doing nothing would prevent her brother from making a terrible match to a penniless nobody. Yet, it also allowed for Mr. Darcy to possibly fall into the woman's clutches. Or the other sister, Eliza, who was apparently on death's door. While Caroline felt superior to Jane Bennet in every way that mattered, that risk was one she could not take. And once she married Mr. Darcy, it wouldn't matter who her brother married. She quickly calculated the eldest Bennet daughter was the least repulsive in looks, temperament, and status. She would do for a sister-in-law if she had to choose one.

"We should go tomorrow while Mr. Darcy is away fetching his physician," she said, feeling powerful again. It wouldn't matter if she was truly kind or not on the visit, just the mere act of doing so would show Mr. Darcy that she, too, took her duty as a member of higher social standing seriously. In fact, she resolved then to always refer to the family as the poor, unfortunate Bennets from now on.

“Good, I shall go with you. You made an excellent point that Mr. Darcy has regularly visited. Perhaps we can take them a gift,” he mused.

Caroline Bingley snapped her hands to her hips and stared at her brother with disdain. "Don't be ridiculous, what could we possibly give them? New pairs of dancing slippers?" she asked comically, still aggrieved that her newest pair was entirely ruined from the mud and muck after the fire. Still, she had managed to escape without injury. Their sister Louisa had been jostled and startled, and taken to her bed claiming her condition required she rest.

"Now you are being ridiculous, Sister," Mr. Bingley stated, walking away from her to avoid revealing anything more about his dealings with Miss Bennet. "I don't know their sizes."

CHAPTER 4

Four days after the fire, Mr. Darcy again called on Longbourn. The household that was once silent as the grave and deep in mourning, bustled with activity. One of the Bennet sisters practiced piano, albeit not very well, somewhere on the first floor. For numerous minutes after being welcomed in the housekeeper, Mr. Darcy and Dr. Stevens stood dumbstruck by the number of household members who passed them without a second glance.

The two youngest Bennet daughters giggled as they came down the stairs to see the visitors waiting for Mr. Bennet.

"So good to see you again, Mr. Darcy," one said, bobbing a curtsy that Mr. Darcy returned with a silent nod of his head. He grimaced as he could not properly recall which sister was which, apart from Jane, and he craned his neck to see if she might be coming to rescue them from their awkward position.

"If you're here for Jane, you're too late. Mr. Bingley is with her in the parlor," the other sister stated, narrowing her eyes in careful observation of the tall man from London.

Mr. Darcy cleared his throat at the surprising information that Mr. Bingley was present. Still, he settled on a way to address the young girls without needing a name.

"Pardon me, but would you be so willing as to find your father? We are here to see him."

The taller Bennet sister made a face.

"He won't like that," she started, pointing down the hall to where the study was which Mr. Darcy was very familiar with. "He never comes to get visitors. If people are welcome, they know where to find him."

Mr. Darcy groaned. He was quite familiar with the strange behavior of his host, but had believed the lack of greeting and social graces before to be the result of the dire circumstances from the fire. He looked to his friend, Dr. Stevens, who stifled a laugh at Mr. Darcy's predicament.

"And forgive me for speaking without an

introduction, Miss?" Dr. Stevens asked the sister he believed to be younger because she was shorter.

"Catherine. Catherine Bennet."

"Don't put on airs, Kitty!" the other sister said, flippantly.

Dr. Stevens ignored the sibling rivalry. "I am looking for a Miss Elizabeth Bennet. I am told she was gravely injured in the fire."

"Oh, Lizzy, yes, but she's all better now. She's playing chess with Papa," Kitty Bennet explained, again pointing down the hall the same as Lydia had done just before.

The two men shrugged and supposed the housekeeper at least by now had alerted Mr. Bennet as to their arrival. Without thinking about it, Mr. Darcy glanced over his shoulder at the closed doors of the parlor, wondering if Mr. Bingley was in fact visiting with Miss Bennet and how very odd the entire household was every time he visited.

After knocking on the door, both men entered the study to find the younger Bennet sisters were in fact correct. Mr. Bennet and his second eldest daughter were playing chess. Mr. Darcy stood arrested by the sight of Miss Elizabeth so entirely lovely, sitting in the sunlight from the early afternoon in the window seat, her legs propped along the cushions with the game table obscuring them from view.

"Mr. Darcy, forgive me, I must not stand," she said with a laugh and Mr. Darcy stood there dumbstruck by the tableau.

Beyond an uncomfortable silence, Dr. Stevens jostled his friend to break him free of his stupor. Swiftly, Mr. Darcy turned to his physician and introduced him.

"Yes, I traveled to London to fetch my personal physician, Dr. Stevens. To help, help," he gulped and finally looked again at Elizabeth, "you heal."

"Well, that is very thoughtful of you, sir," Mr. Bennet exclaimed, jumping from his chair to shake the hand of the man who had rescued his favorite daughter. "When we had not seen you in a few days, I worried that you no longer enjoyed my company!" Mr. Bennet teased, earning a sudden bewildered look from Mr. Darcy. Dr. Stevens grinned at the expense of his friend as he lifted his doctor's bag and took a few steps towards his patient.

"Miss Elizabeth?" he asked, bowing his head

until she acknowledged his presence. "Frederick Stevens. Might I see the injury in question?"

Sighing with consternation, Elizabeth began to lift the edge of her gown, wincing at the fresh pain of pressure against her injuries.

Dr. Stevens began to protest, looking back to Mr. Darcy, "Perhaps Madam, that is—"

"Oh your friend cannot claim false modesty now, hand him a copy of *Hamlet* to calm his nerves," Elizabeth said, gritting her teeth through the pain of reaching down to lift the soaked bandages from her badly blistered skin.

"Hamlet?" the doctor asked, confused, until the sight of the injury attracted his full attention. The skin above Elizabeth's ankles bubbled in a devilish red with numerous bulging blisters.

"My God, we must lance these immediately!" he cried, looking back to Mr. Bennet and Mr. Darcy.

Elizabeth protectively waved her hands over her skin, shaking her head.

"Mr. Jones was very explicit that I am to leave them be," she said.

Mr. Bennet frowned.

Dr. Stevens protested. "Mr. Bennet, the risk of infection is quite high with burns this extensive. I have seen too many a maiden scalded by the stove on a Monday, well by Wednesday, in the grave by Sunday."

Mr. Bennet closed his eyes.

"Are you insinuating I am at risk of dying, sir?" Elizabeth asked with her eyebrow raised. She didn't want to insult Mr. Darcy's friend and physician, but truly she had been burned before in her life. If she was a foot away from death's door, then so were the lot of them!

Dr. Stevens nodded gravely. "'Tis a tragedy, but it happens."

Mr. Darcy cleared his throat.

"In my own household."

Mr. Bennet nodded understanding as the pallor of his family's would-be benefactor paled most noticeably.

"Ah, that is why you hurried so fast to London."

"But Papa, Mr. Jones—"

"Who is Mr. Jones?" Dr. Stevens interrupted.

Mr. Bennet eyed his daughter and looked down at the unveiled blistering skin. Mr. Jones' treatment had carried her thus far, and she was very much back to her old spirits by any account.

"You've truly seen people succumb to burns this late?" he interrogated Mr. Darcy.

Mr. Darcy swallowed hard the lump in his throat. "Too often. It's a wicked false hope."

Mr. Bennet turned back to Dr. Stevens and gave a quick nod.

The man took off his coat and handed it to Mr. Darcy, then pointed to the chess pieces for silent permission to move them.

Elizabeth protested.

"Mr. Jones is our local apothecary and he saved me, I'll have you know," she began to plead, looking to her father. When Dr. Stevens pulled out what appeared to be a long hairpin with a garishly jagged tip, Elizabeth grew agitated and tried to leave. "Father, this is madness. If we must do this, let me retire to my room. Jane will assist me," she bargained as it was one thing to humiliate Mr. Darcy as he had humiliated her, but quite another for him to witness the horrific display of fluids leaving her person.

Mr. Bennet stepped forward and pressed a firm hand to Elizabeth's shoulder to still his daughter.

"Be brave, my Lizzy. If you cannot bear to look . . ." he said, offering his handkerchief to her but she waved it away as Dr. Stevens seemed fully prepared to begin the procedure.

Dr. Stevens pushed his spectacles up that had slid down his nose, leaning closer to inspect the largest blisters. "If the liquid is clear, we have caught it in time."

"And if it's not?" Mr. Bennet asked.

Dr. Stevens didn't say anything but rolled up his sleeves to get to work. Elizabeth watched the first puncture, that felt like a sharp prick, and then nothing. The pressure of the cloth applied to catch the oozing liquid stung severely to the burned skin around each blister. She sucked in her breath and turned away, cursing an oath against her own pride. Her foolishness to run back into that building had saved no one and she suffered acutely for the folly.

Opening her eyes as Dr. Stevens and Mr. Bennet spoke on the condition of the fluid, Elizabeth caught the eye of Mr. Darcy. The man had hung back to the middle of the room. The most vulgar display of the procedure remained shielded from him by the backs of the two men administering the treatment. But his eyes were not in that direction at all, but squarely staring at Miss Elizabeth's face.

She again found herself lost in the brown, pained eyes of a man who stood nearly as a mystery to her. Yes, she had been foolish to run into that fire to seek her sister, the same sister escorted out the back by Mr. Bingley it turned out. But what had been his aim?

Elizabeth found herself no longer registering the pricks and prods. Her body numbed the response as it had since she ceased taking the laudanum. Pain functioned in that way for her, a mild nuisance to her that would send her sisters howling. She watched Mr. Darcy's face and smirked. The man had insulted her nearly to her face and then risked his life for hers.

Just as the last blister had been lanced and Dr. Stevens offered a numbing balm for her afflicted skin, the study door opened and Mrs. Bennet entered in a gown newly dyed black.

"Mr. Darcy! So good to see you and your . . . " she trailed off, as she could not at first place the man sitting next to her husband. "Friend," she finished, unsure how to mark the man's identity. "Will you be joining us for dinner?"

Flummoxed at Mrs. Bennet's sudden request contrasting with her attire, Mr. Darcy did not offer the woman an immediate answer.

Dr. Stevens put away his ghastly instrument of torture. "They may fill with fluid once more. Each time, you must lance it. Do not let the fluid build up."

Elizabeth looked down at the doctor's handiwork immediately repulsed by the sight. Her skin once strained and stretched by the size of the blisters was now marred by large flaps of translucent skin hanging limply where the largest blisters had been. Quickly, she covered her wounds with her skirts, seething at the flicker of pain from the touch. To her surprise, the constant ache of pressure was gone, and she looked at Dr. Stevens with a new appreciation.

"Will you be staying for dinner?" she asked the doctor who had aided her affliction, against her better judgment.

"I believe we are to stay at a place called Netherfield Park? It is not far from here, I am to understand," Dr. Stevens explained to his patient.

"You ought to stay here, in case Elizabeth has any ill-effects. May I persuade you to trouble our guest room?" Mr. Bennet asked. "We shouldn't need it for at least another fortnight," he added.

"I am . . ." Doctor Stevens looked to Mr. Darcy for assistance in what he should do, and to his surprise, Mr. Darcy nodded. "I am delighted by the invitation. Let me have my things removed from the carriage," he said, standing up to leave the study.

Mr. Darcy turned around to Mrs. Bennet, and

accepted the hospitality. Then to the woman's surprise, he walked across the room to take the chair in the corner closest to Elizabeth, and began to set up the chess board once more.

Finding she wished to know more about this man who ignited her senses, confounded her expectations, and irritated her thoughts, Elizabeth addressed him. "Do you play, sir?"

"Indeed. I am sorry we spoiled your game with your father."

"Hopefully, I will benefit greatly from it," she said, nodding towards her feet. "Would you like to play a game?"

Mr. Darcy offered a thin smile. "It would be my honor."

"Lovely, so long as you don't mind moving my pieces," she said, holding up her gloved hands. "They are still painful to use."

Mr. Darcy agreed that he did not mind moving Elizabeth's pieces to the squares she called out, and to a passerby, it appeared that Mr. Darcy was playing a game all by himself. A few moves in, and he quickly realized Elizabeth's skill surpassed his usual opponents, including Mr. Bingley and Dr. Stevens.

"How often do you play, Miss Elizabeth?"

She uttered the directions for her knight to

take one of his bishops. "Father and I play a few games per day, " she said, feeling the heat of a blush as he responded to her play by moving his rook. She sighed and ordered a pawn to the final row on his side to get back her queen. "I also solve the chess puzzles in his weekly sporting paper when he cannot. Check."

Mr. Darcy smirked as he tried to escape her clutches. "It's rare for me to meet a lady who would feel no compunction about boasting better wits than her father," he commented and Elizabeth laughed.

"Queen to F7, check mate. And I don't boast that I have more skill, Mr. Darcy, for the man taught me."

Mr. Bennet came over to inspect the board after his daughter's dazzling display of warfare. "She holds an infinite amount of patience and youthful exuberance, as well. Sometimes an old man just can't be bothered with a puzzle of meaningless solution."

"Again?" Mr. Darcy asked and Elizabeth, stifling a yawn, agreed then said after the next game she would need to retire to prepare for dinner.

This time, Mr. Darcy took the position of aggressor, and Elizabeth found herself struggling to parry his attacks. She wished to focus on the game, but she was beginning to feel the exertion of the day draining her, loathe as she was to admit that she needed to rest. Mr. Bennet left the study for a few moments, with the door open, to help his wife settle Dr. Stevens into his room. As Mr. Darcy swapped one of his pieces for hers, he found the courage to ask her a question he had been meaning to ask for days.

"Why did you run back into the assembly rooms?"

Elizabeth caught his stare and lost her ability to breathe for a moment. When she inhaled deeply, her normal answer of saving Jane just didn't seem to suit the real question he was asking. The one he really wanted to ask was why was she so different from all of the other ladies that he knew. Likewise, she wanted to know why Mr. Darcy was so different from the other gentlemen she knew. It took Mr. Bingley days to come and see if Jane was well.

Just like their chess match, where she realized her error was three turns before and there was nothing she could do to save herself, she turned the question back on him.

"Why did you run in to save me?"

He acknowledged the silent understanding

they now held between the two of them, survivors of a great tragedy, bound by the unthinking actions of each other. Instead of giving her a swift answer, he moved another piece, also recognizing the game was mated in just a few moves. They were both spared further clarification by Jane and Mr. Bingley who had wandered and found them in the study.

"I heard you had arrived, straight from London," Mr. Bingley pronounced with a sound of shock to his voice. Elizabeth tilted her head towards Mr. Darcy, rather baffled the man hadn't stopped at Netherfield Park before visiting.

"If the good doctor is finding his moment to refresh himself," she offered, "do you need to return to Netherfield Park before dinner?" Elizabeth asked. But Mr. Darcy shook his head, rather uncomfortable at the sudden interest into his well-being. The man shifted his weight in his chair and set the abandoned game aside.

"We stopped the village before Meryton now that the inn . . ." he began, and then stopped as all four of them could not quite accept the tragedy that had befallen the village less than a week ago.

"Jane, how did you escape?" Elizabeth asked, suddenly realizing that during her recovery, no one bothered to fully explain how foolish her folly had been.

Jane blushed. Mr. Bingley blushed. Elizabeth looked to Mr. Darcy for an answer but he was just as confused as she was. Believing her to be asking him a silent question, he answered the obvious:

"I had run in after you, I did not look for Miss Bennet."

The air hung with silence until Elizabeth prodded her sister again. This time, gesturing with her gloved hands to urge Jane to speak. The physical reminder of her sister's injuries appealed to Jane's sense of guilt.

"I was dancing with Mr. Bingley," she started and Elizabeth rolled her eyes.

"Yes, yes, and I was dancing with Mr. Lucas —" Elizabeth gasped, suddenly fighting back sobs as another part of the night flooded her memory. Her voice choked out to a whisper, "Charlotte?"

To her surprise, Mr. Darcy reached out and gently touched her arm, close to her elbow in comfort. When she looked down at his hand, he immediately withdrew it.

"I'm sorry, Lizzy, she did not survive," Jane said.

"Nor did her sister," Mr. Bingley added, earning an incredulous stare from both Jane and

Mr. Darcy. "Oh, my apologies, I should have considered . . . "

Elizabeth began to struggle with her emotions as the night played out in a ghastly memory. Fuzzy images of laughing at Mr. Darcy's arrogance, the context so wholly meaningless now. Then they were all dancing in a circle, taking turns, and someone yelled "Fire!"

Gasping for air to breathe, Elizabeth hyperventilated as she finally remembered spying Charlotte's body, unmoving in the smoke and oppressed by the heat. She felt as though she were there again, resigned to meeting the same fate. Only she hadn't.

Finally, Elizabeth counted to five as the others called her name and steadied her breath, then braved looking to her right at Mr. Darcy, the man who had saved her from a certain death of her own making. Crushed by the debt she owed, his presence brought to mind too many things at once. Why had he risked his life for a foolish woman he barely knew? Why was he here, and as Jane recounted, at their home every chance he had until she woke up? As her head throbbed in pain, from the crying and overthinking, new voices joined the study.

"Lizzy! Lizzy!" her mother called out.

Doctor Stevens pushed Mr. Bingley aside to get closer to Elizabeth. He pressed his hands to her forehead which was burning up with fever.

"She is ill," he pronounced and suddenly Jane and Mr. Bingley left the small room so that Doctor Stevens and Mr. Darcy could help Elizabeth stand up. When the sudden change in position made her feel lightheaded, she staggered a moment and it was quick action by the two men grasping her arms that kept her upright.

"Darcy?" his physician inquired.

With a whisper to her ear begging her forgiveness, Mr. Darcy placed one arm across the back of her shoulders and the other under her thighs to effortlessly scoop her up. Feeling safe and secure, Elizabeth wrapped one arm around his neck.

Mr. Bennet appeared cross, but did not further his daughter's indignity by trying to take over carrying her above stairs. He commented on the convenience of young men when ladies swoon, trying to avoid the seriousness of the development.

"Send for Mr. Jones," Elizabeth muttered.

Mr. Darcy shushed her as he wordlessly carried her to the room he knew to be hers from before. After laying her chastely upon the bed, he was shooed away by Jane as she worried at how vulnerable her sister was in such a state.

Mr. Darcy nodded and realizing that he could not bear to see her again in pain, retreated from the room. Dr. Stevens remained behind with Mr. Bennet and Miss Bennet.

CHAPTER 5

Mr. Darcy found Mr. Bingley down in the parlor, pacing before the fireplace.

"Perhaps we should stay another night for dinner," Mr. Darcy suggested.

Mr. Bingley ran his hands through his hair, highly agitated about what he had just witnessed.

"Can you leave her in this state?" he asked, but Mr. Darcy remained stoically still. So Mr. Bingley implored him further, stepping close enough to his friend for a physical confrontation if necessary. "Darcy?" His friend turned away. "Darcy! I don't know what you are playing at. I merely helped Miss Bennet out of the inn—"

"So that is why she did not wish to answer?"

"I did nothing ungentlemanly! I certainly didn't carry her out for the whole world to see!"

"Charles," Darcy warned, calmly, "please lower your voice. We can discuss this elsewhere," he said, suddenly fearful of one of the younger sisters lurking about and spying.

"You're the one who always warns me not to show any certain preference. To not raise hopes." Mr. Bingley stormed away to the other side of the room. "Even when this time, it's I who desperately hope . . ."

As Mr. Darcy stared at the back of his friend, another had joined the parlor without a word. But it was not one of the sisters.

"Gentlemen."

The strange tone of Mr. Bennet captured the attentions of Mr. Bingley and Mr. Darcy. The two would-be suitors ceased their friendly discussion about the Bennet sisters to give their host proper respect.

"I will not mince words, much as my wife would like me to say otherwise than what I am about to say. The circumstances of your acquaintances with my daughters are unorthodox, to say the least. And not unlike times of great war, it is reasonable for young people to believe themselves wholly in love with someone they just met when the fragility of life is suddenly threatened by immediate danger."

"Sir," Mr. Bingley began, but Mr. Bennet held up a hand.

"I do not doubt your sincerity or intentions towards either of my daughters, I simply ask that this is not the time."

Mr. Bingley nodded, but Mr. Darcy could not so easily agree.

"What do you believe to be our intentions?" Mr. Darcy asked, earning a laugh from Mr. Bennet. The man continued to laugh as Mr. Bingley shook from nerves and Mr. Darcy stood stoically still.

"Darcy, you cannot claim you do not hold esteem for Miss Elizabeth," Mr. Bingley outed his friend, without speaking about himself.

"As I have not declared or requested any meeting with Mr. Bennet on the matter, I feel it is within my right to inquire as to what the man expects of me," Mr. Darcy stated, not bringing up his or Elizabeth's feelings on the matter.

Mr. Bennet walked further into the parlor, away from the door.

"I'm afraid it's rather plain that you both have traveled to a foreign county and found yourselves captivated by a stock of young lady they don't breed in London drawing rooms. But if either of you press your suit now, you will forever wonder if your acceptance was on your merits or merely the romantic fantasies of young ladies who identify with a novel's heroine."

"Do you think so little of your daughters' ability to comprehend and have good sense?" Darcy asked.

The elder man grimaced.

"To you, sir, I could deny nothing that you ask of me. You have restored my greatest treasure, and even now, I am a poor man trading on your generosity. But no, it is not Lizzy's good sense and comprehension that I am worried about." Mr. Bennet bowed his head to Mr. Darcy, but then looked him directly in the eye to underscore the severity of the matter at hand.

"You doubt Miss Bennet then?" Mr. Bingley spouted, dumbly, and Mr. Darcy scolded his friend, still locked in a staring contest with Mr. Bennet.

"No, Charles, he doubts us."

Mr. Bennet did not contradict Mr. Darcy's assessment and instead held up his hands open and empty in front of him, as though to weigh two arguments. The pantomime made Mr. Bingley calm down, as he was always quick to find a congenial resolution. Mr. Darcy clasped his hands behind his back, the same hands that carried the woman he knew very little, not once, but twice. The first time he had barely registered the feat, this last time, he felt devastated to leave her in the care of others.

"What would you have us do, then?" Mr. Bingley pleaded, and Mr. Darcy closed his eyes in annoyance.

This was not a negotiation Mr. Darcy wished to have when he was still unsure of his own thoughts on the matter. Mr. Bennet's sage advice, from such an unlikely source, challenged his own behavior. Did he hold intentions towards Miss Elizabeth? He knew what his irrational emotions felt when he spied her running back into that building. He didn't question that he had acted any greater than another gentleman might act.

But then to see her fighting spirit, and quick mind, had allowed himself to believe his first opinion had been in haste. He had answered Charles at the assembly with a selfish unwillingness to concern himself with the needs of others in a moment of his own discomfort. Yet, Miss Elizabeth had played chess with him, when she was likely in a great deal of pain, for his comfort in an awkward social situation.

Darcy suddenly realized he had been asked a question when Mr. Bingley called his name.

"I apologize, I was not attending," he said, asking for them to repeat what was decided.

"Mr. Bennet wishes for us to see the ladies at services and then call later that week," Mr. Bingley said.

"But Miss Elizabeth . . ." Mr. Darcy cleared his throat and stopped himself as what he was about to say was so wholly inappropriate for a man unconnected to the lady. He tried to think of better words to express his worry, and then realized such a worry mattered not if it came to fruition. If Miss Elizabeth did not recover from her burns and affliction, then she would be lost to him forever and no decision need be made.

Mr. Bennet narrowed his eyes at the wealthy man from Derbyshire. "I am certain your man, Stevens, will keep you apprised of my daughter's condition. And I did not say you may not call," he said, to Mr. Bingley. "I ask that you do so with the same circumspection and restraint that you might have employed if there had not been a fire. And also, to please consider that my wife is mourning her sister."

Mr. Darcy nodded in agreement, with only one other concern in his mind. "Will you speak to

Mrs. Bennet or your daughters about our discussion here tonight?"

Mr. Bennet made a horrified expression of disgust as the sound of heavy footsteps came down the stairs, signaling they were soon to be joined by others. Dr. Stevens rejoined the men and closed the parlor door behind him.

"She sleeps. And Miss Bennet sits with her," Dr. Stevens explained.

Mr. Darcy wanted to ask more questions, but a swift glance by Mr. Bennet held his tongue.

"Is there any way to know?" Mr. Bennet asked. Dr. Stevens shook his head.

"No, the night will be telling. We will know more in the morning," Dr. Stevens said.

Mr. Bennet used the finality of Dr. Steven's prognosis to bid Mr. Bingley and Mr. Darcy a good afternoon, not saying a word that echoed their previous discussion. Mr. Darcy checked once more with Dr. Stevens if he was comfortable staying at Longbourn and his old friend and personal physician laughed.

"You forget that I'm a doctor even when you don't need my services."

"Yes, yes, but I am also newly acquainted with the Bennets," was all Mr. Darcy would say.

Dr. Stevens clapped Mr. Darcy on the

shoulder as they walked out to the carriage ready to take them to Netherfield Park. Mr. Bingley's horse was tied to the post position to be led back home as well. "If they attempt to harm me, I will be sure to send word," he said jokingly as the two forlorn suitors had to retrench.

They were a quarter of a mile down the road before Bingley began to needle his friend again.

"So we can call tomorrow?" he asked.

Darcy pinched the bridge of his nose, suddenly feeling inordinately exhausted by the day's events.

"What happened while I was away to London?" he asked.

Bingley recounted how he had first visited with Caroline, and they stayed for the afternoon playing cards in the parlor with Miss Bennet and Miss Lydia. Then Miss Bennet had to tend to her sister. Instead of leaving, Mrs. Bennet asked them to dine, and Miss Bingley said she had to leave for a previous engagement with her sister.

"But I was not aware of any engagement, so I returned Caroline home and then I came back for dinner."

Mr. Darcy groaned.

"You did not notice that Mr. Bennet had not invited you to dine?"

Mr. Bingley shook his head. "Hardly saw the man, he was upstairs most of the time or went to his study."

"And then today?"

"Oh, Caroline complained of a headache, so I called alone. About an hour before you arrived."

Mr. Darcy started to place the puzzle pieces in place and felt an enormous amount of sympathy for Mr. Bennet, though truthfully the man was partially to blame for the problem. If he was playing chess with Elizabeth most of the day, and the household didn't announce Mr. Bingley's arrival due to the man's eccentricities, or Mrs. Bennet's scheming, it was little wonder the man asked for space.

"If we call tomorrow, it will be for a brief moment to inquire as to Miss Elizabeth's health and we will remain outside."

"Outside?"

"Yes, outside. Though I am certain we can contrive some errand to run in Meryton."

Mr. Bingley brightened. "Yes, I can talk to Mr. Phillips about extending the lease."

"The man who just lost his wife?"

"Oh." Mr. Bingley suddenly appeared crest-fallen. "I don't understand, are they going into mourning?"

"What do you not understand?" Mr. Darcy asked his friend.

Mr. Bingley stared out the window. "When my mother died, my father continued to work. There were orders, the factories. And when he died . . ."

"You sold the factories."

Mr. Bingley watched the passing trees along the road, starting to grow familiar with the way between the two estates, his leased one and Longbourn. "Up North, there isn't time to mourn. There's no time to live, either."

Mr. Darcy nodded, finally grasping where his friend's faux pas derived from: he was raised in trade.

If Darcy had been honest, he was also not sure of the practices and customs in the area, as mourning in the countryside was similar to that in a factory town. Some work simply can't hold off. The only place he'd seen structured mourning was in London, and not among anyone who worked for a living. Or didn't need to hastily marry to shore up debts left by the deceased.

"You're entirely correct, Charles. There is little to understand in any of this. But time rarely weakens a decision. We will honor Mr. Bennet's request," Darcy said, as the carriage came to a stop.

"That's easy for you to say, your lady won't be working side-by-side with Dr. Stevens," Mr. Bingley pouted.

Mr. Darcy chuckled for the sake of his friend, but still could not laugh fully. His heart was in too much agony, praying for hope that Elizabeth lived. That became his silent prayer to the Almighty as they trudged up the steps to the front doors. Even if Elizabeth did not return his affection, or his affection became false and a traitor to his integrity, that it be God's will for the lady to live.

CHAPTER 6

The first day the men contrived to call on the Bennets, it rained. Therefore, there could be no standing outside and the roads were too wet to risk a carriage. Miss Bingley fretted about Mr. Darcy catching a cold, and he laughed in spite of himself at the worry. It just so happened his personal doctor was only a short distance away. Still, a note sent from Longbourn to Netherfield Park that afternoon communicated very little had changed.

The next day, Mother Nature again refused to cooperate. The only good news that day claimed Miss Elizabeth's fever made her sleep more often than not, but she tolerated broth and tea and remained conscious. At her insistence, Mr. Jones was summoned and Dr. Stevens was not at all impressed with his abilities.

Darcy read line by line of the missive, over and over again to try to find some clue about her feelings towards him. But alas, Dr. Stevens wrote as a clinician, not an agent of cupid. He discarded the letter to the fire with the paltry four lines memorized.

"There you are, Mr. Darcy. However did you find this room?" Caroline Bingley announced upon intruding on his solitude.

Disliking artifice of any kind, he did not want to lie. He would insult his hostess by truthfully claiming he had endeavored to find a room away from her. At one point, he considered asking a footman to move a desk into his suite of rooms, an idea he now wished he had not abandoned so quickly.

"I found it perfectly positioned in equal distance to the library and stables," he commented, pulling out parchment to busy himself. He had finished the letters of business, a task he set to complete before learning Miss Elizabeth's condition in case he was needed. But he was not needed. Nor requested.

Without thinking, he began a letter to his sister, Georgiana. He had promised to tell her of his trip and had not written since the afternoon of the assembly. Dipping his quill into the inkwell, he began his letter by assuring her that he was healthy and well and that it pained him to tell her of the great tragedy he had witnessed.

"I am so grateful to have found you alone, sir, because I believe we should discuss the poor, unfortunate Bennets." Caroline glided directly to the side of his desk, standing closely over his shoulder. Darcy put down his pen and pushed the chair back a considerable distance to reduce the intimacy.

"Would this conversation not be better with your sister, Mrs. Hurst? Or your brother?"

"But that's precisely who sent me! My sister! My brother will not hear sense! Do you know he has designs to ask for Jane Bennet's hand in marriage? Can you imagine? He's only known the woman for a week!"

Mr. Darcy frowned. He did not like Miss Bingley's rational argument against Mr. Bingley's attachment most importantly because it echoed arguments against his own. "We've been acquainted with Mr. Bennet from the start of our stay, he was one of the first neighbors to call if I recall. And Mr. Bingley met her uncle some months ago in securing the lease," Mr. Darcy pointed out.

Caroline scoffed. "And what has that to do with Miss Bennet?"

Mr. Darcy chuckled and returned to his letter to his sister, unbelieving that Miss Bingley could be this dense. "Surely marriage has far more to do with the family and connections a lady comes from than fleeting feelings of attraction. Mr. Bennet is a well-respected squire in this county, Mr. Phillips is the trusted attorney in Meryton."

"Her family is practically penniless. Do you know that when Mr. Bennet dies some distant cousin inherits the entire estate?"

"Ah," Darcy said, thoughtfully, staring out the window as he thought how horrible such a circumstance would be for Elizabeth to lose her childhood home. "That is the way sometimes, even in families of the Ton. The son inherits."

"But they have no son!"

Darcy considered her for a moment, feeling another circumstance similar to the carriage ride with Mr. Bingley. Miss Bingley had never seen an earl or viscount die a premature death and a young wife kicked out of her home as the eldest son from the first marriage took over the title and the purse strings.

"If my own father had remarried, and thankfully he did not, the same practically penniless status would have befallen any stepmother of mine. I was unaware your brother needed to marry for wealth, I should have to ask him how his finances became so dire," Mr. Darcy said, sardonically, trying to go on writing the letter to his sister.

"So you will not help me?" she asked, quibbling her lower lip and her eyes glistening with the beginning of crocodile tears about to fall.

"Caroline!" Mr. Bingley scolded his sister as he entered the small sitting room on the first floor that his friend had claimed in sanctuary. "I told you that Darcy did not wish to be disturbed!"

Caroline turned in a huff and left the room, claiming to need something or other from her sister, Louisa. Mr. Darcy turned back to write more lines to his sister, exalting the eldest Bennet daughters' kindness, social graces, and even mentioning his games of chess with Miss Elizabeth. He did not tell his sister that Elizabeth had bested him, just merely that they had played nearly two games. He was just beginning to mention the situation of her injuries in the most polite fashion possible when Mr. Bingley decided to take the place of his sister in annoying him.

"My man has news from the village," Mr. Bingley began. When Mr. Darcy did not inquire further but continued to write, Bingley continued on. "Before the fire, there was a plan for the Wiltshire militia to winter in the town. Unfortunately, without the tavern, it appears alternative plans have been made. A number of the merchants are quite angry, demanding to know when the tavern will be rebuilt."

Mr. Darcy nodded, pausing his lines to his sister. "What are the plans to rebuild?"

Bingley shook his head. "Sherman didn't know. The family that ran the establishment perished in the fire."

Darcy closed his eyes, recalling the wails and screams of that night. He had heard tales that the children of the inn master had been put to bed before the assembly began. The bucket line had worked nearly until dawn, dousing the flames and then looking for any survivors. Mostly, the men found the lost.

"Tis a tragedy of great magnitude, made worse by the changed plans of the militia," Darcy said.

Mr. Bingley grunted and picked up the ink pot that Darcy used, wrinkling his nose at the smell. Mr. Darcy raised his eyebrows and his friend hastily returned the ink to the desk, cursing that the lip of the glass pot had stained his fingers. Mr. Darcy laughed at his friend.

"I suppose that's one way to earn one's stains," he commented, teasing Charles about how much he despised letter writing.

"Who wants a bawdy group of soldiers in their town? Caused a bunch of trouble is what my father always said."

Mr. Darcy penned a closing paragraph to his sister, employing his mind in two places as he wrote his words, and tried to understand Bingley's opinion. When he could not, he asked him to explain.

"They drank and caroused, preying upon the women," he explained.

"And your father lost more than one worker, I'm sure, to a hasty marriage," Darcy realized, out loud.

Mr. Bingley shrugged.

"The shop owners and tavern appreciated the extra coin the soldiers spent," Darcy pointed out. He sanded the letter and sealed it, adding it to the pile that would need to travel by his personal messenger.

A crack of thunder disturbed the two gentlemen, and another downpour began its angry assault on the land. Mr. Bingley sighed and crossed his arms.

"I suppose that puts a pin to it."

"A visit is out of the question today," Mr. Darcy agreed. He also frowned because the weather would also delay his letters, as he did not wish to risk his staff to the elements unless it was absolutely necessary. But if the rain continued tomorrow, he would have no choice as his home in London and estate in Derbyshire needed his instructions.

"Any word?"

Mr. Darcy nodded. "She is tolerating broth and remains conscious."

"Miss Bennet?"

Mr. Darcy closed his eyes at his friend's helpless state of blatant preference for the fairer Bennet sister. "None, but why would my physician pen an update about a lady we both hope is very well in regard to her health?"

"Of course I do not wish Jane to be ill, I only wondered if Dr. Stevens had anything to say about her. I am happy to hear that he does not."

As the storm continued to rage outside, Mr. Darcy's muscles began to feel tense and out of sorts with his lack of physical activity in the last few days. Not wishing to play yet another game of billiards with Bingley, he offered another suggestion for them to pass the time.

"Fancy a bout of fencing?" he asked, with a wry smile.

Mr. Bingley brightened at the suggestion but pointed his finger at his friend. "I shall most assuredly lose as I do not have your reach. But I suppose I do owe you practice with as much as you have humored me at billiards."

"So long as we are not playing cards again with the ladies, I am an eager participant."

Bingley laughed. "No, no, swords it shall be. Meet in the ballroom in a quarter-hour?"

Mr. Darcy agreed, and the two restless gentlemen of Netherfield Park found an engagement for their frayed nerves.

CHAPTER 7

Elizabeth Bennet heard humming. The constant, irritating humming that she could not escape courtesy of the care of Dr. Stevens. Reluctantly, she opened her eyes to see the man inspecting her chamber pot, making that infernal noise.

"Sir, I believe I was quite clear last evening that I would prefer you not enter my bedroom before I have awakened," she said, pushing up to her elbows, looking around for Jane. Her bedroom door was open and she could hear numerous voices of her family members throughout the house. "Where is Jane?"

Dr. Stevens made notes in his journal and restored the handkerchief placed over the private vessel. "She just left to see about your tea. This is yours?" he asked, and Elizabeth flopped back on the bed in defiance.

"Yes. As I told you yesterday morning, my sister has her own."

"Quite right, quite right."

"Father!" Elizabeth shouted, truly at the end of her patience with the good doctor Mr. Darcy had sent to vex her night and day.

Dr. Stevens chuckled. "He is not in," he explained, suddenly earning a glare of threatening anger from his patient. Stepping cautiously back from her bedside, the man wisely returned to stand in line with the open door. "Perhaps I should step out and allow you to dress?"

"Yes, and close the door on your way out!" she shouted, waiting until the door latched before daring to remove her coverlet.

Sucking in her breath in preparation for pain, Elizabeth gasped when removing the coverlet no longer bothered her legs! She laughed almost maniacally as she flapped the blanket over and up, over and up, with no ill effects.

After her amusement faded, she gazed down at the tops of her feet and wrinkled her nose. The skin still looked terrible where her burns had been, but after five days of vinegar treatments from Mr. Jones, and weathering a fever for three, she finally felt only the echoes of pain where once it had caused her to howl.

The lack of pain allowed her to exuberantly leap from the bed, only for her weakness from a lack of food to cause her to collapse with a thump. She cursed her thoughtless behavior but righted herself out of sheer determination.

"Miss Elizabeth!" Dr. Stevens' voice called and he began to open the door.

"I am well! I am well!" she shouted, her voice cracking from a touch of dryness. Feeling as though she ought to wait for Jane, she called the next best thing and asked the good doctor to send her a maid. Elizabeth despised help with her dressing, as in her earlier years the staff were always loyal to her mother and tattled on her about many a torn petticoat and muddied hem. But the new maid, Henrietta, had become a close ally now that Elizabeth and Jane enjoyed control over their pin money.

Jane arrived with a tray of tea and toast just as Henrietta struggled to fix a gown over Elizabeth's undergarments. The fabric bulged and creased unflatteringly along the bust line. Over a week without indulging in her favorite foods had thinned her form to practically Jane's measurements. In the end, such a solution was her elder sister's idea: Elizabeth would borrow one of Jane's frocks for the day.

"Would I be a horrible sister if I begged we take the tray downstairs? I am so tired of this room!" Elizabeth complained, sitting on the bed with her feet dangling over the edge. Her skin healed and closed, she could wear regular stockings and slippers for the first time since the dance. And her hands no longer hurt where the glass had cut them, the scars just as Mr. Jones said, on the inside of her palms and out of sight.

"I have a better idea," Jane said, with a cat-like grin. She walked over to the door and opened it, revealing Dr. Stevens waiting in the hall. "Did I not hear you speak to Mr. Darcy and my father this morning that if Elizabeth is well, you must return to London?"

Dr. Stevens walked in and bowed to both ladies. "Yes," he said, sheepishly. "This is why I was trying to conduct my final examination. I believe you to be well . . . quite well," he emphasized, using Elizabeth's own words she had uttered over and over for the last two days.

Still, Elizabeth fumed. In her opinion, that man was the very reason she had taken such a turn for the worse. And without Jane, no one would have called for Mr. Jones. As far as she was concerned, not only could Dr. Stevens leave Longbourn, but she hoped she never saw the man again!

Stalling, Elizabeth utilized the tray Jane had brought up to make herself a cup of tea. The water had cooled in the time it took from its arrival to her partaking, providing the perfect amount of warmth to her parched throat from a combination of slumber and recovering from the infection.

"Lizzy?" Jane asked as her sister showed signs of thoroughly enjoying the doctor's discomfort.

"Jane, I am breaking my fast. And after I will happily go below stairs to speak to Father and Mr. Darcy, assuming the man is still here."

"He is," Dr. Stevens explained.

Elizabeth brushed an errant curl that had fallen to her face. In her haste to be dressed, she had not pinned her hair properly.

"Perhaps you'd care to wait downstairs?" Elizabeth stated more as a demand than a question.

Dr. Stevens walked over to her bedside table to retrieve the last of his instruments and place them into his leather bag. Elizabeth refused to meet the man's eye, earning a soft sound of disapproval from her sister.

Once they were alone, Jane assaulted Elizabeth's behavior.

"You know, many people have nursed you back to health," she began.

"Not him! He nearly killed me!"

"Lizzy, you are being ridiculous."

"Until I was under his care, I was mending well."

Jane placed the slice of toast with a pat of butter on a plate and handed it to her sister. If she was so intent on breaking her fast, Jane intended to help her.

"That is entirely unfair. Even Mr. Jones said that there was no way to know when your body had begun to fight infection. Dr. Stevens might have saved you! If he hadn't drained that fluid, you might have succumbed!"

Elizabeth scowled. She sipped her tea to hold back what she wanted to say to Jane, that it was easy for her to not be cross, she hadn't been subjected to the burning cleanse of vinegar treatments every few hours to an open wound. As she allowed the unsweetened, bitter liquid to stun her taste buds, Elizabeth watched Jane more closely. Her sister looked almost as terrible as she felt. Her eyes were darkened circles, her lips thin and cheeks pale in color.

But any sympathy Elizabeth might have felt for Jane ended the moment her elder sister decided to help her with her hair. It was always clear when Jane was angry and the last activity you wanted her to do was brush or style your hair.

"Ow! You're hurting me!"

"Tosh, you cannot go downstairs with this tangled mess of a bird's nest," Jane charged, insulting Elizabeth's curls that rarely submitted to being tamed.

Closing her eyes, she felt Jane's efforts slacken in pull. Her sister attempted to be more gentle.

Elizabeth sighed.

"What do I need to say in Father's study?"

Jane didn't answer at first. So Elizabeth asked her again.

"Well, Mr. Bingley and I were taking a turn around the garden when Father and Mr. Darcy spoke. I only caught the end of the conversation."

"Jane!" Elizabeth expressed her frustration with her sister. For two decades, at least since they could both talk, they had looked out for one another. Elizabeth helped Jane escape their father's notice when it came to lessons, and Jane distracted their mother whenever Elizabeth's exploits were cause for admonishment.

Jane mumbled as she held the pins in her mouth while putting a simple plait into Elizabeth's hair. One by one, she pulled out the pins to weave and push them into place, taking care not to poke Elizabeth's scalp. Still, she missed once.

"Use a ribbon," Elizabeth pleaded, but Jane told her it was too late. Elizabeth moved away just as Jane finished her handiwork.

Taking the empty teacup from her sister, Jane set it on the tray.

"I'm certain if you wash your face and muster what spirit you can manage, you will say and perform everything you need to convince Mr. Darcy and Father that you no longer require Dr. Stevens' services."

Elizabeth raised an eyebrow at her sister as Jane seemed to be in great haste to finish her duties to her sister.

"Mr. Darcy? I surely do not need to humor his opinion on the matter," she said, with as little care to her voice as she could playact.

"That tone will work well with them, but will never persuade me," Jane said, laughing lightly at her sister. "I heard the name you moaned in your sleep," she added, cheekily, grabbing the tray and leaving the room before Elizabeth could protest.

Vanity seized control over Elizabeth's

thoughts as she consulted the looking glass that hung over the dressing table she and Jane shared. The reflection staring back at her shocked her. She had thought Jane looked poorly, she looked positively ghastly! The grayish sunlight spilling into her room from the mid-autumn morning made her coloring appear ghoulish. Gone was the strong, vivacious woman who hiked more mornings than not up to Oakham Mount. Her cheekbones were suddenly very prominent, as was her collarbone. Twisting her mouth this way and that to make faces in the mirror, Elizabeth settled on the only happy thought she could muster before facing both her father and Mr. Darcy together. At least now her mother would not scold her for eating extra biscuits at tea time in consideration of her figure!

CHAPTER 8

Gliding down the stairs, Elizabeth paused on the landing to look out the oeil-de-boeuf offering a perfect view of the front lawn of Longbourn that led further to a grazing pasture. Walking down the drive was her sister, Jane, on the arm of Mr. Bingley, to take yet another turn in the garden.

Elizabeth at once felt jealous that Jane had abandoned her so swiftly, but then smiled as the couple turned and she spied her sister laughing. Mr. Bingley made Jane laugh, and seeing her sister's happiness banished away any ill feelings.

Calling on this happiness, Elizabeth walked with more energy than she truly felt and entered her father's study after giving the door a strong, sound knocking.

"Elizabeth," her father said, surprised to see his daughter.

"As I was saying, I believe she has made a full recovery—" Dr. Stevens continued his report and only stopped when Mr. Bennet held up his hand.

"Good morning, Papa. Dr. Stevens," Elizabeth made each a small curtsy and then turned, "Mr. Darcy." As she closed her eyes to curtsy once more, she hesitated a moment as she felt slightly light-headed, but steeled herself to keep to her performance.

"My dear, I did not intend for you to get out of bed," Mr. Bennet chided, moving to Elizabeth's side to inspect her most closely.

Utterly annoyed and beyond patience at being inspected, prodded, and treated, she stood on her tiptoes to gawk at her father in the same manner he was in disbelief over her condition. She pantomimed a funny little dance as he tried to walk around her, but she turned to keep her face squarely on his.

"Father, I am well."

"That is what you said the day Dr. Stevens arrived," Mr. Bennet reminded her.

Frustrated, Elizabeth retreated from her father and took a seat in her favorite place by the window. She could see Jane and Mr. Bingley had walked around the house already and were clearly in her view. Jane spoke animatedly about some subject and Elizabeth tried to read her lips, but she was speaking too fast and giggling for Elizabeth to make out a word.

Mr. Darcy cleared his throat. "May I get you anything for your comfort, Miss Elizabeth?" he asked.

Elizabeth turned to catch his gaze, intending to act like she had forgotten he was there. But she had not forgotten. If she hadn't survived the incredible pain of an inferno, she would have thought her skin was on fire anew. Instead, she knew it to be the traitorous response of her heart and body to the man she knew so little about. Even Dr. Stevens had been unhelpful when she had tried to ask him more about Mr. Darcy.

"Are you chilled?" he asked.

"No," she replied. "I am quite warm."

"And well, she is quite well, in my professional opinion," Dr. Stevens added.

Elizabeth suddenly realized there was something else going on. "Dr. Stevens, do you have another patient in London that you left to tend to me?"

All of the men in the room focused their attention on Dr. Stevens, who began to stutter slightly.

"Stevens?" Mr. Darcy asked, and the poor doctor nodded.

"Father, what feat must I perform to prove to you that I am well? A sprint to Netherfield Park and back? Shall I lift a carriage with my bare hands?"

Mr. Bennet held up his hands in surrender and flopped into his chair behind his desk. "Peace, Lizzy, at least I know your sense of humor has returned, even if you look as though you could use three good meals."

Elizabeth smirked at her father's comment about her appearance, a face that made Mr. Darcy stifle a laugh.

This made her attention fall to Mr. Darcy. "Sir, please release Dr. Stevens from my care. Settle what matters are between you and know that even if I should fall ill again, we have a most capable apothecary, not a half-hour ride. Besides," she said, reaching out with her healed, ungloved hands, for the small chess table. "I owe you a game."

Mr. Darcy stood facing Elizabeth with his back to Mr. Bennet. Catching Miss Elizabeth's eye, he involuntarily licked his lip, earning a gaze of incredulity from Elizabeth that made him thrilled he could shock her as easily as her behavior often shook him.

"I should be honored to play again if that is permitted?" he asked, turning to receive a nod from Mr. Bennet.

"Yes, yes," he said, waving off Mr. Darcy while an errand boy brought a stack of letters to the study. Mr. Darcy saw Dr. Stevens out and Elizabeth busied herself with setting up the game. Opening one of the missives, her father scanned the lines and began to shout.

"That fool! I said do not come!"

"Father?" Elizabeth asked, gently, as Mr. Darcy and Dr. Stevens had not gone far and she didn't want them to hurry back in if the news was unpleasant.

Mr. Bennet held the folded piece of parchment and checked the timepiece he wore chained to his vest. "Franny!" he shouted, rising from his desk and leaving Elizabeth to her confusion and chess pieces.

For a few moments, she sat pleasantly patient for Mr. Darcy's return. But a few minutes turned into ten, then ten turned into nearly a quarter-hour. Unwilling to go out and see what was taking so long to dispatch Dr. Stevens from their midst, Elizabeth stood up to find a book on her father's shelf. She recalled that he once owned a tome on chess puzzles and decided she could amuse herself while she waited. Spying the worn, green cloth book she was sure was the title up high on a shelf, she stood on her tiptoes. Reaching up for the book, she discovered it was just out of her grasp.

"Allow me," a deep, baritone voice offered, his hand lightly brushing hers as he brought the book down. Elizabeth felt a jolt of passion when her skin touched his and she pulled her hand back as though it had been scorched. Turning around, she was staring directly into the chest of Mr. Darcy, watching his cravat rise and fall with each breath the man took.

"Thank you," she managed, tilting her chin up to see his face more clearly. She marveled that like her, he appeared to have been spared any kind of pox marks, and his jawline stood in stark contrast to the longer sideburns he sported. The proportions of his forehead, nose, and lips were what she would have dearly loved to paint as they were nothing short of beautiful in her opinion. And his eyes, always slightly sad and searching, for what she could not decide. But when she looked directly at him, she felt exposed as though he could see all of her down to her very thoughts.

Nodding his head, he took a step back and looked down, allowing Elizabeth to slip by him and back to the window seat.

"Could you look out the door and see if you spy a maid or footman?" she asked.

"You do not have a bell system?" he asked, looking around the study.

Elizabeth laughed. "Not in here, my father won't allow it," she said, her stomach rumbling to remind her that she had given it precious little in the way of sustenance. "As you offered earlier, I would like a tray of food and tea," she said, suddenly realizing that she was asking Mr. Darcy, a man she was told had an income of over £10,000 per annum, an order like he was a common hallboy!

"Of course, you must be famished. I once was ill for a week and thought I could eat an entire buffet upon my recovery," he related, before going to the doorway and then stepping out until he discovered the housekeeper, Hill, and made the request for Miss Elizabeth.

Feeling impressed by his manners, when he returned, she held out her hands palm down with two pawns, one of each other color, in them. He clasped his hands behind his back and appeared to inspect them very closely as he made his decision.

"And did you?" she asked.

"Did I what, Miss Elizabeth?"

"Eat an entire buffet," she reminded him.

"Err, no," he said, with a blush, before tapping her right hand. She opened it to reveal a black pawn, enjoying the easy time she had with this man.

As he plucked the piece from her palm, he suddenly spied the angry red gash that raced from one edge of her pinky finger to her thumb.

"For a sister," he whispered.

"A folly," she replied, cross with herself. Shaking the offending hand as she tucked it away, out of view.

Without another word, Mr. Darcy sat down and their game commenced. After a few moves, he realized that Mr. Bennet was not back. So he politely inquired as to the man's whereabouts.

"Has your father abandoned us? Are we finally receiving the treatment of your sister and Mr. Bingley?" he asked, in a conspiratorial whisper. He worried that insulting her father's chaperoning skills might offend her. But Elizabeth's foot gently nudged his boot, and she apologized for the affront. Then she counter-attacked with a bishop.

"He opened a letter, called someone a fool, and then went in search of my mother."

"Ah," Mr. Darcy said, reaching for a piece, then pausing to think better of it and placing his finger to his lips to think. Elizabeth watched his mannerisms with such interest, she began to wonder what his lips would feel like if she touched them with her fingertips. Would they be smooth and velvety, as they appeared? Or dry and leathery from the harsh sun?

"It is your move," he politely pointed out as he caught Elizabeth staring directly at him.

"Yes," she said, looking down at the board and trying to realize what piece he had moved. She blinked a few times and couldn't bring her mind to the task at hand, finding herself suddenly overwhelmed by the man's presence.

"Mr. Darcy! Mr. Darcy! How fortunate you have not left us yet, sir! You owe us a dinner, you do!" Mrs. Bennet barged into the study with Mr. Bennet close behind her.

Both chess players abandoned the game to witness the comedic sparring of Elizabeth's parents.

"Madam, I merely asked you about dinner this evening. I did not ask for us to hold a dinner."

"But you said we should have guests!" she

countered, and Mr. Darcy and Elizabeth exchanged glances.

Mr. Bennet closed his eyes and laid the piece of parchment Elizabeth saw him leave with on top of the desk. "No, I said we would have an unexpected guest."

Elizabeth could not resist her curiosity. "Who? Who is our unexpected guest?"

"His cousin! The one who will throw us all out when Mr. Bennet dies. But Lizzy! Lizzy!" Mrs. Bennet cooed, rushing to the desk to lift the letter and read it for herself. "He writes that he was most troubled by news of the fire and comes earlier than planned to offer consolation and," she paused for dramatic effect to read the line she was most affected by. "He finds the settlement of the estate to be a great hardship for his fair cousins and comes with hopes of admiring one of you!" she finished, clutching the letter to her chest and looking up at the ceiling as though her prayers had been answered.

Elizabeth gulped and silence hung in the air of the study, sucking away all of the joy she had felt just a moment before.

Mrs. Bennet abandoned her silent murmurings of thanksgiving and then looked directly at her daughter. "You, Lizzy, you are the most clever.

He is a parson and you will be sure to catch his interest," she said, bustling over to her daughter to urge her to stand up. Noticing Jane's frock, she scowled. "Oh, but not in this color, it's more suited to Jane. You should wear a lovely shade of brown, dear, to appear modest."

Mr. Darcy cleared his throat, watching as Elizabeth, horror-stricken, looked to her father for intercession. He waved his hands.

"Your mother has declared you must live here forever, my Lizzy. Who am I to contradict her?" he asked, pouring himself a healthy amount of port.

"Oh, Mr. Darcy, sir, you and Mr. Bingley are most welcome to dinner. I shall be able to balance out the table then, you see," Mrs. Bennet explained.

Watching Elizabeth get practically dragged out of the study, interrupting their game once more, at her mother's insistence, he sat dumbstruck by the lack of argument from Mr. Bennet.

"I beg your pardon, sir," Mr. Darcy began, in earnest.

Mr. Bennet smiled, sipping his port.

Mr. Darcy suddenly felt his mouth run dry as he tried to process what had just transpired. One moment, he was blissfully unaware of the world around him, in the presence of Elizabeth, who bewitched him body and soul. The next, she was whisked away, and he held many questions for Mr. Bennet.

"Cat take your tongue?" he taunted.

Miss Bennet and Mr. Bingley entered the study, in another repeat of their ill-timing from before.

"Gentlemen, I believe my daughters have enjoyed your company and look forward to your presence at this evening's dinner," Mr. Bennet supplied the farewell that neither Bingley nor Darcy wished to hear.

"Dinner?" Mr. Bingley asked.

"Yes, yes, a grand fete I am to believe to welcome my cousin. The heir presumptive, probably hoping I died in the fire."

Jane gasped, but Mr. Bennet winked at her. "And please, invite your sisters and Mr. Hurst," Mr. Bennet instructed Mr. Bingley. "I will make sure that Mrs. Bennet is aware they are to come."

Jane looked for Elizabeth, and not seeing her, looked to Mr. Darcy for an explanation. Despite the man's stony expression, he glanced up at the ceiling to signal to the observant Miss Bennet where to find and hopefully rescue her sister.

"Goodbye, Mr. Bingley. Thank you for the

walks, they were most invigorating," Jane offered, giving a curtsy before hurrying off to see her sister. Hearing her mother's voice above stairs, Jane abandoned all pretense of a ladylike cadence, lifting her skirts so as not to trip on the hem.

"There, you see," Mr. Bennet said, escorting the men to the front door. "My girls have much to do it would appear. We shall see you no sooner than seven o'clock this evening," Mr. Bennet warned.

"So late?" Mr. Bingley asked, disappointed that Jane did not offer him one last forlorn look before leaving.

"Must give our newest guest time to settle himself, Mr. Bingley. Not everyone agrees so well with travel," Mr. Bennet stated, reminding the young man that his cousin was likely not of the same means and mode that Mr. Bingley and Mr. Darcy enjoyed.

When finally alone back in his study, Mr. Bennet could hear the heavy footsteps and bustling activity that reminded him of the night of the assembly. Straightening the miniatures of his daughters on his desk, a present from Elizabeth one Christmas, he sighed as he steadied the one of his Lizzy. She had perfectly captured her look of disdain that he knew so well from their hours together.

"Which will it be, my clever girl? The best your Papa can offer to you or the delights of Mr. Darcy? Hmm?" he asked, as though the portrait could answer back. Reading again his cousin's missive, he cursed the man Collins for arriving a whole week earlier than they had previously agreed. His letter about the fire had intended to put off the visit, not hasten it.

Still, perhaps the man would be a good match for one of his daughters and fix the largest regret of his lifetime: that he was without the means or discipline to properly protect his daughters after his demise.

When another loud crash came from above stairs punctuated by his wife's shrill voice yelling commands, Mr. Bennet poured himself another drink. Mr. Collins of Hunsford Cottage held no chance of leaving Longbourn without marrying one of his daughters if his wife had anything to say about it.

CHAPTER 9

Enlisting the aid and attendance of Miss Bingley required an act of subterfuge. The Hursts politely declined the dinner invitation, sending their regrets that Mrs. Hurst was feeling unwell.

Caroline tried to employ the same ruse against the obligation, but Mr. Darcy preyed upon her baser nature. Quietly, he promised to observe the Bennet family more carefully and hear her objections with an open mind. She giddily agreed to attend the dinner then, and Mr. Darcy hoped the loss of a couple would not thwart Mrs. Bennet's careful plans too drastically.

What Mr. Darcy did not count on was Caroline complaining during the entire carriage ride over to Longbourn.

"What will you do, purchase that drafty, leaky estate? You will have to put more money into it than what it's worth, won't he Mr. Darcy?" She countered her brother who had just extolled the graces of Jane Bennet and announced his plans to ask for her hand in marriage that very evening.

"It is not so bad as all of that," he said.

"No, it's worse. Half of the chimneys pour smoke into the room if you attempt to use them! Louisa and I cannot open the windows in our suites. The sash in Mr. Darcy's room leaks!" Caroline enumerated the problems with Netherfield Park, all common problems for any home that sat unattended for a span of years.

"Surely every house has its issues. As an owner and master, that is what you do, Caroline. You repair and make improvements, securing your legacy," Bingley said, arguing back with his sister the very words they heard their father say over and over again. It was John Bingley's dearest wish for his daughters to be raised as ladies and for his son to buy an estate. The work of generations was a never-ending sermon in the Bingley household.

Mr. Darcy closed his eyes and thanked Providence that although his sister Georgiana had recently given him some trouble on a holiday to

Ramsgate, though the disaster was averted due to her good nature and proper behavior, she never raised her voice like Miss Bingley. He wasn't entirely certain how Charles abided the snipes and complaints of his younger sister, but not wishing to ruin his appetite with indigestion, he tried to put an end to the sibling squabble.

"Tomorrow, let us ride out together, Charles, and we will inspect the property. If you are considering an offer of purchase, at least have valid information or confirm the information that Phillips gave you," Mr. Darcy suggested.

"And then you will tell my brother how unsound his plan is," Caroline urged.

"Caroline!"

Mr. Darcy blanched as the space was entirely too small for them to both be yelling at each other. He lowered his voice to barely above a whisper, questioning how he had ever come to place himself in this situation. But Bingley had been of such a service to him to avoid the higher social circles since inheriting Pemberley, and Darcy genuinely enjoyed his company, he couldn't fault the man. "Your brother's decision is his own. But please, both of you, my head is beginning to ache."

After suffering the sudden concerns by Miss

Bingley for his health, the last of the short carriage ride to Longbourn was quiet.

Upon entering Longbourn, however, the chaos of all five Bennet sisters; a new acquaintance, the aforementioned fortunate cousin; Mr. and Mrs. Bennet; and the grieving Mr. Phillips stunned the arriving Netherfield Party as soon as they were shown into the parlor. There was scarcely any place to sit, so Mr. Darcy found a close corner to stand in.

Introductions were made, and no sooner had his name been pronounced, than Mr. Darcy found himself suddenly receiving the very low bow of Elizabeth's tall cousin.

"Mr. Darcy! Of Derbyshire and Pemberley?" The man asked as soon as he rose again.

"Yes," Mr. Darcy said, cautiously, offering the man a slight nod of his head in polite greeting.

"William Collins, at your service, sir!" he exclaimed, promptly bowing once more even lower. Mr. Darcy frowned, until he caught the tinkling sound of Elizabeth's giggle from across the room, and looked up to share a look with her in solidarity. The cousin had been quite close to her when they entered the room but suddenly shifted allegiance upon hearing Mr. Darcy's name.

"Forgive me, but are we acquainted?" Darcy asked.

"Not formally, most certainly! But I am well-versed with your virtues, sir. I am parson to your kind, wise, and most gracious aunt, Lady Catherine de Bourgh! I am happy to say that I left her in the best of health and spirits not two days ago, and your intended, Miss de Bourgh, was very well, as well," Mr. Collins said, loudly.

Mr. Darcy sneered at the man before him. "I beg your pardon, but Miss de Bourgh is not my intended," he said, sharply in a hoarse whisper.

"Quite right, Lady Catherine told me your alliance was of a particular kind, not yet announced," Mr. Collins said conspiratorially, winking at Mr. Darcy. He turned around to look at Elizabeth Bennet on the settee talking with Miss Bingley. "An alliance I hope to model myself. Yes, yes, families such as ours should strengthen our roots from within, would you not agree?"

Mr. Darcy panicked for a moment as he worried that Elizabeth might have heard her bombastic cousin. However, she playfully spoke to Miss Bingley and her grieving uncle on the other side of the room, and he felt relief. Not wishing to speak to Mr. Collins anymore, but finding his other preferred people engaged, he walked away to stand closer to Miss Elizabeth.

Unfortunately, Mr. Collins followed him there like a lost puppy.

Caroline Bingley believed she had attracted Mr. Darcy over through her display of kindness, and so she laid her condolences on thickly. "Mr. Phillips, I am so sorry for your loss. How wonderful it is that you can seek solace in the bosom of your dearly departed wife's family. It is such a poor, unfortunate circumstance," she said.

Mr. Phillips stared blankly into his teacup. "Magdalene loved socializing," he said, with a sniff. "Our home is so quiet without her," he managed, emotion choking in his throat.

Mr. Darcy watched the man closely with great sympathy for his situation. He had felt wrecked the nights he worried that Miss Elizabeth might not survive and as he risked a glance to the crown of her head, his eyes flicked involuntarily to the rather felicitous view of the lady's bosom, restrained tightly in her gown to boost her cleavage to the greatest advantage. Shaking off his inappropriate stirrings, he opened his mouth to say something polite but was usurped by Mr. Collins.

"At least you can take solace in your children," Mr. Collins said.

Mr. Phillips looked up with his tormented, red-rimmed eyes, gaping at Mr. Collins.

When her uncle could not speak, Elizabeth gently interceded.

"You are thinking of my mother's brother and his wife, in London. My Aunt and Uncle Phillips had not yet been blessed with children," Elizabeth said, giving her uncle a strained smile of empathy.

"No, I'm sure they have four children," Mr. Collins said, looking to Mrs. Bennet for support.

Elizabeth pinched the bridge of her nose and Mr. Darcy almost laughed as he identified so wholly with the sentiment of her body language.

"Can you not offer the man words of comfort from the Almighty?" Mr. Darcy asked, thoroughly put off by the man of the cloth, even if he was Elizabeth's cousin.

"Yes, yes, that is, in times like these, my patroness, the great Lady Catherine de Bourgh, says that we must be grateful in our suffering, so that, that is, our suffering is paramount to our future suffering when—" Mr. Collins struggled until Mr. Darcy finally interrupted him.

"Hear my prayer, O Lord, and give ear unto

my cry; hold not thy peace at my tears: for I am a stranger with thee, and a sojourner, as all my fathers were."

Mr. Darcy's rich tone silenced the other conversations in the room and nearly all had to turn to him as he looked most intently at Mr. Phillips.

The aggrieved widower softly thanked the stranger from Derbyshire and Mr. Bennet used the pause to encourage everyone to the dining room. Hoping to catch Elizabeth for a brief moment, Mr. Darcy was again thwarted by his aunt's sycophant.

"Cousin Elizabeth, may I lead you into dinner?" Mr. Collins asked.

Under the stern eye of her mother, Elizabeth sighed and accepted the offered arm of Mr. Collins without argument.

CHAPTER 10

Mr. Darcy blinked as he watched Elizabeth leave without even looking back at him. He caught the eye of Mr. Bennet across the room and heard an echo of the man's words in his head.

In front of him, Mr. Bingley escorted Jane into the dining room and Mr. Darcy began to wonder if he was entirely mistaken about Miss Elizabeth, perhaps she did not hold any particular regard for him. A tug on his coat sleeve attracted his notice. Miss Bingley gazed expectantly up at him, waiting for him to offer to escort her. Feeling trapped, Mr. Darcy spied a quick alternative.

"Mrs. Bennet, may I be so bold as to offer you an escort into your lovely dining room?"

"Mr. Darcy! My, this is unexpected," she said,

looking at the clearly disappointed Miss Bingley and making a quick calculation. "Yes, that is very kind sir, and you shall sit next to me. Since the poor Hursts will not be able to join us this evening, we shall have their places removed from the middle."

Unfortunately, this left Mr. Bennet to escort Miss Bingley, and he graciously led her to her chair, next to Mr. Darcy at his wife's end of the table. At the other end, Mr. Bingley and Jane and Elizabeth and her cousin Mr. Collins sat closest to the head. Even worse luck was that he was seated on the same side of the table as Elizabeth and Mr. Collins, so not only could he not hear their conversation, he could not even see her for the majority of the meal except for passing glances. Yet, any time he leaned forward or tried to attend to the conversation down at that end of the table, he never could seem to catch her eye as he had in the parlor.

Miss Bingley asked the rudest questions of Mrs. Bennet, and the woman lapped up the attention, divulging the most embarrassing personal details. Jane apparently had suitors before, some gentleman who wrote her poetry. When Mr. Bennet died, they would all share an income from her meager settlement of £400 per annum for all six of them if interest rates remained steady.

"But it shan't come to that, I think," Mrs. Bennet said, drinking her wine.

"Do you have a family estate or some other means of rescue?" Miss Bingley inquired in a voice dripping with false sincerity.

Mr. Darcy felt the food in his stomach somersault, increasing his discomfort tenfold.

Mrs. Bennet laughed.

"No, my family is from trade, same as you," she said, almost making Mr. Darcy choke on his wine as he wished he could turn and see Miss Bingley's face at the 'friendly-reminder.' "But look down the table, your brother and Jane are most assuredly half in love with each other, and my clever Lizzy has caught the eye of her cousin who will inherit everything. We shall be quite fine, indeed, but what about you my dear? You must have had two or three seasons in London by now?"

Mr. Darcy coughed as the meat pie he had taken a bite of to avoid adding to the conversation became stuck in his throat as he tried to laugh and chew at the same time. Miss Bingley motioned for a footman to pour him more wine, and Darcy could barely breathe as he coughed and coughed until finally, a large mouthful of wine pushed down the dry pastry and large chunk of stewed meat.

Before Miss Bingley could answer, a sharp tinkling sound of silverware striking glass ceased all conversation at the table. All eyes turned to Mr. Collins who struggled to push back his heavy, oaken chair that had been a fixture at Longbourn for generations. Still, the man managed to scrape it against the rug in the time of only a few giggles from his youngest cousins, sitting across from Mr. Darcy. Then he stood.

"I lift a glass, to the family of Bennet, our host, my relations, and soon, I hope to call something even more tender," he began, looking down at Elizabeth sitting next to him. "I have heard of the incomprehensible tragedy that has befallen this hamlet and thanked our merciful God that my cousin, Mr. Bennet, was spared."

"I bet he did not," Mr. Darcy said, under his breath.

"And to my dear Cousin Elizabeth, who took it upon herself to try to rescue more the night of the fire, suffering great pains in her efforts, spared from certain death by a hero amongst us, to you, Mr. Darcy!" he shouted, raising his glass further and causing all attention to be on his patroness' nephew at the opposite end of the table. Mr. Darcy avoided their stares but tried to find one. Only she refused to look his way and instead contemplated her hands in her lap.

"I should not have known what a debt I might owe you, sir, upon hearing of your impeccable character and good judgment, I was quite aware. And I shall happily carry back to your most prestigious aunt all that I have learned here of your selfless behavior," Mr. Collins finished.

"To Mr. Darcy!" Mr. Bingley added, causing everyone to raise their glasses in a cheer. Elizabeth also raised her glass but remained focused on her sister across the way.

"That was lovely Mr. Collins. Is there anything else you'd like to impart? Hmm?" Mrs. Bennet encouraged.

Mr. Collins gaped his mouth open and closed like a misplaced fish upon the land. Sensing an opportunity, Mr. Bingley pushed his chair back without the same difficulties as Mr. Collins. He raised his wine and looked lovingly next to him, beginning to extoll the virtues of Jane.

"I would like to say that Miss Bennet has captured my heart—"

"That's quite enough! Dinner is at an end." Mr. Bennet said, leaning over to Mr. Bingley, whispering something in his ear. Mr. Bingley turned a deep shade of red, and chaos erupted at the table.

Mrs. Bennet began to fuss at her husband, while Lydia Bennet and Kitty Bennet complained that they had not finished eating and wanted dessert. Mr. Darcy tried to keep up as many began moving in the dining room all at once: Mr. Bennet and Mr. Bingley going one way to his study, and Elizabeth scurrying over to her sister, Jane.

"Now will you help me? No one in their right mind would join this family," Miss Bingley said, through clenched teeth.

When Mr. Darcy turned his head for a moment as Miss Bingley had again pulled on his arm before she spoke, he lost sight of Elizabeth. Servants began clearing the dishes and then started bringing them back as Mrs. Bennet gave a conflicting order.

When he tried to find the two eldest Bennet daughters, he was left wanting. Somehow, they had disappeared from the dining room completely. A tap on his shoulder startled Mr. Darcy and he pushed his chair back to rise, practically squashing Mr. Collins against the wall.

"My apologies," he offered, moving the chair so that Mr. Collins could escape.

Mr. Collins tugged on his simple parson's coat, setting aside the injury to his dignity.

"I should see to my cousin, I feel," he began, looking towards the back door that Mr. Darcy knew led towards the staircase.

A surge of jealousy coursed through Darcy's veins as he despised the very idea of Mr. Collins sleeping under the same roof as Elizabeth!

"She is with Miss Bennet, and while I am certain you have secured Mrs. Bennet's good opinion, may I offer a small piece of advice?" Mr. Darcy asked, watching the buffoon drool over his every word.

"Any guidance your illustrious person would grant me I would be most gracious to accept, sir."

Mr. Darcy schooled his reaction to mask his intent of leading Mr. Collins astray.

"Seek out Mr. Bennet's approval. He is the head of this household and if your aims are as you say, to repair the great breach between the branches of your family long ago, make him your ally." Mr. Darcy hoped that Mr. Bennet would at least be equitable in his treatment of suitors for his daughters' hands: unhelpfully equitable.

Mr. Collins brightened and smoothed his hands over his chest with pride. "Yes, that is most excellent advice, thank you!" And he then sauntered towards the eastern side of the home towards the study.

Mr. Darcy, unfortunately, was torn between what to do. He wanted to go to the study and be a part of the discussions behind that closed door but knew Mr. Bingley would tell him all. He also did not trust himself to remain calm and sensible when that oaf of a parson spoke as though an alliance between him and Elizabeth was already formed.

Presented with no better options, Mr. Darcy resumed his seat and ate what he could of his meal. He continued to hope that Miss Bennet and Elizabeth returned to the dining room, but there was nothing he could do to put such a plan into motion.

As Mrs. Bennet prattled on and on about Mr. Bingley most assuredly working out details of an engagement with her husband, she drank more wine than was sensible. Miss Bingley began a discussion with the younger Bennet sisters across the table about the latest fashions, enjoying their rapt attention as she described various gowns she had worn and seen in ballrooms.

"Are there ladies who wear all white and drench their fronts with water to make the fabric sheer?" the second to youngest Bennet sisters asked.

Mr. Darcy could not believe his ears and looked to Mrs. Bennet or Mr. Phillips to discipline their charges. But no rebuke came. Without a thought, he demonstrated the same tone he used with Georgiana when she would need a verbal correction, rare as it was.

"Such a topic should never leave the mouth of a lady, most especially in mixed company," he scolded.

To his surprise, neither Mrs. Bennet nor Mr. Phillips took the opportunity to reinforce his chastisement and the two younger Bennet sisters made faces at him. The middle daughter, the quiet one, nodded enthusiastically at him.

"I have told you, Kitty, and you too, Lydia, that you are dangerously flirting with the path of a fallen woman," she added.

Mr. Darcy cringed. In the misguided attempt to shepherd her younger sisters, Mary Bennet had introduced an even worse topic to the table.

"Mrs. Bennet," he began, praying that if he changed the subject, he could avoid another uncomfortable subject. "Forgive me if this pains you, but I was not well-acquainted with your sister. Can you share more about what she was like? With your consent, of course, Mr. Phillips," he said, nodding to the sad, silent man who sat as almost a hollow shell of a person.

"Maggie was my eldest sister and always quick to make new friends. Why when we were growing up in London, she knew all of the best parties and dinners to attend. . ."

For the better part of half an hour, Mr. Darcy listened patiently to Mrs. Bennet recount how her sister's romance with Mr. Phillips, meeting him when he was a student, led her to move to Meryton. Visiting her sister one summer, she met Thomas Bennet, the son of the local squire who despised the idea of his son marrying anyone considered beneath his station. The Bennets had been attached to Longbourn for generations, back to the days of Plantagenet mischief under various surnames, but it was the current Mr. Bennet's father who insisted on the entail. Knowing his son to hate all matters of estate management, he feared that Mr. Bennet would sell Longbourn and move to London.

"So we married and I was so young, what did I care about a document insisting I would bear his son?" she asked, sloshing her wine goblet freely.

The three remaining Bennet daughters

watched their mother with their eyes widened in equal measures of shock and trepidation.

Suddenly, Mrs. Bennet began to sob. Mr. Phillips stoically rose from his seat and set a hand on his sister-in-law's shoulder.

"Girls, perhaps you ought to retire," he said, gently.

Mr. Darcy and Miss Bingley took this moment to give their thanks for the meal and made their way back to the parlor to wait for Charles. The evening, intended to welcome a new relation to the neighborhood and grant a grieving man a well-cooked meal with family, was an unmitigated disaster. The Netherfield party had been the interloper. Darcy suddenly felt very ashamed of himself for accepting the invitation. Before the arrival of Mr. Collins, the family had little choice but to encourage any would-be suitor that presented himself. But now that the heir presumptive was happy to marry one of the daughters, the pain and fear of ruin that had haunted Mrs. Bennet for the last decade and a half since she birthed her last surviving child could be eliminated. If only she was not also dealing with the untimely loss of a most beloved sister.

"These people are in pain, we have trespassed," he said, softly.

"I am the one in pain," Caroline Bingley whined. "Where is Charles?"

No sooner had she wondered about her brother than the study door far down the hall opened and Mr. Bingley walked in a daze to the room. They accepted their outerwear from the butler and waited as their carriage was fetched, offering a ride to Mr. Phillips who declined, stating that he would stay the night.

For once, the carriage ride back to Netherfield Park was silent as Mr. Bingley sat gazing out the window up at the full moon. When they reached their temporary home, Miss Bingley complained of a headache and retired straight away. Finally alone with Mr. Bingley, it was now Mr. Darcy who was so desperate for information.

"What did you decide with Mr. Bennet?" he asked, straight to the point as his head ached as well from the evening's tumultuous entertainments.

Mr. Bingley gave his friend a lop-sided grin as though he were the cat who caught the canary.

"He has accepted my request to court Miss Bennet, so long as we do so at their home and my own, chaperoned, of course, but not out in public, for not less than six weeks." The man used his fingers to recount the various stipulations placed upon him, happy he was able to recount them all.

Mr. Darcy furrowed his brow as Mr. Bingley bid him a good night and made silly, shuffling dance-like steps to the stairs, talking to himself. He could not imagine if he was ready to ask for Mr. Bennet's approval for Elizabeth's hand in marriage, finding cause to celebrate a courtship that was over a month and a half long. Two months if one included three weeks for the banns to be read. Then again, it wasn't Mr. Bennet's approval he craved at all. It was hers. And no matter how long her approval took to secure, Fitzwilliam Darcy would burn with desire.

CHAPTER 11

"If you wish to avoid Mr. Collins, you have to dress so we can begin," Jane Bennet whispered into her sister's ear. Her proximity playfully tickled her sister, and Elizabeth squirmed.

Suddenly remembering the night before, Elizabeth sat bolt upright in the bed, nearly bashing her head into Jane's face who jumped back just in time.

"How do I sleep so much now? We have reversed roles," she said crossly, getting up from the bed and searching for a gown and her favorite boots. Jane laughed at her sister who indeed, before the fire, was so often up early to stomp in the woods with her sketch book in hand.

"You dress, I will make sure the wagon is packed and father knows where we are going."

Elizabeth flailed her arms to shove her frock over her head. "Bring Marcus. William is too slow," she said, giving her preference of driver to accompany them on visiting the tenant farmers.

Traditionally, they delivered baskets the morning after the assembly, but the fire had dictated otherwise. Still, for Elizabeth, the prospect was absolutely thrilling. It would be her first outing in almost two weeks. Jane had already delivered half of the baskets on the side of their father's lands that buttressed Lucas Lodge. This morning, they were working towards the west.

After making herself ready, Elizabeth used the back stairs to leave through the kitchens. The unsuspecting staff grinned and greeted the Bennet sister they saw most often. Hill approached Miss Lizzy to offer her a slice of toast with honey butter wrapped in a handkerchief.

"Miss Jane has a jug of warmed cider for you, and the other food Cook packed. This is something just from me," she said, with a wink, compressing her hands around the outside of Lizzy's as she accepted the bundle of fabric.

"Thank you, I am so happy to bother you all

again," she teased, as kitchen maids scrambled with their early morning chores. Most of them wore cast offs from Elizabeth and Jane's closets, apart from the gowns passed down to their younger siblings. But Lydia and Kitty had begun demanding custom frocks now that they were out and socializing, a new burden upon the family ledger.

The wagon waited for Elizabeth, full of a half dozen baskets and her sister Jane, with the stable hand William at the reins. The previous evening's dew clung to the bottom of her cloak and underskirts as she clasped her hunter green cloak around her shoulders, pulling the hood up as the chill prickled her sensitive skin. Accepting a hand from her sister, Elizabeth grinned as she pulled herself up into the seat next to Jane.

William tapped the crop and called out for the two horses to begin driving the wagon to the backroads that criss-crossed the Bennet property.

Jane leaned over to talk privately to her sister. "Father said take William or you could not go."

Elizabeth pursed her lips, and the three ducked their heads low as an unruly branch threatened to knock into their heads.

"Must talk to Mr. Harper about that one," William muttered, and the girls agreed.

The first farm they visited was the closest to the main house. The Altons were a good family of six with two of the children grown and on their own. The best situated, from generations of working the land at Longbourn, their eldest daughter had just taken a maid's position at Netherfield Park when Mr. Bingley came to the neighborhood. Still, the Bennets put together a leg of salted ham and jars of the jellies made that summer from the berry gardens to aid the family's coming winter.

Two houses later, and the morning sun finally appeared over the trees, giving Elizabeth a proper bathing in her outdoor sanctuary. She turned her face up to the powerful rays allowing the sway of the wagon to lull away the stress of every matter waiting for her back at home. Squirrels raced along the nut trees planted in the front pasture of the Moran family. When the front door was not opened, William carried the basket to the back to find anyone in the barn. This basket was much bigger than the previous, as Mr. Moran had grown ill and passed away the previous winter, so the farm was now managed by the Widow Moran and her eldest son, James.

Jane had remained uncharacteristically quiet during most of the morning, and Elizabeth suddenly thought it best to ask her about Mr. Bingley.

"Are you cross with Father about last evening? I do think Mr. Bingley was about to propose," Elizabeth said.

"He already has," Jane answered softly, looking around her to make sure they were truly alone. But the only sound was an angry duck quacking at another duck threatening his territory in a nearby pond.

"Jane!" Elizabeth exclaimed, but her sister hushed her. Still, Elizabeth gripped her sister's arm and implored her to tell her more. "How? When?"

Jane gave her sister a sly smile.

"What happened between you two the night of the fire ?" Elizabeth asked, recalling the other day when the fever came upon her, both Jane and Mr. Bingley avoided her questions entirely.

"Our dancing party separated. You and our sisters and Mr. Darcy all followed the flow of people to the front of the tavern. Mr. Bingley grabbed my hand and led me towards the back, where there were less people. But I slipped," she explained, "and then suddenly there were too many people, oh Lizzy, it was horrible. Part of the upper level collapsed into the kitchens," Jane said, closing her eyes.

"We all saw too much that night," Elizabeth said, sagely.

"Yes, but we survived," Jane said meekly, receiving an affirming nod from her sister. The annoying duck had waddled from the pond and began babbling his quacks around the wheels of the wagon. Both of the Bennet sisters laughed at the silly animal's antics, until it hid under the bed of the wagon.

"Oh no, shoo! Shoo!" Elizabeth said, holding onto the wagon and leaning over to scare the duck away. Her head upside down, the duck looked defiantly at his would-be villain with a proud side eye and emphatically quacked!

"Lizzy!" Jane reached over and dragged her sister back into a seated position. "If you fall out of this wagon and hurt yourself again, so help me I will not call Mr. Jones but let you suffer," she chastised.

Elizabeth giggled at her sister, finding Jane so markedly changed since the night of the fire. Large gaps existed for Elizabeth in witnessing her sister's transformation, due to her recovery. But Jane's new strength in voicing her needs delighted her. "So when did Mr. Bingley ask you to marry him?"

"After I kissed him."

"After you— you—, not you, no, never," Elizabeth could not believe she heard her sister correctly. "Jane, you didn't!"

Jane suddenly appeared stricken with shame, then nodded. "He pushed people aside, hard Lizzy, and helped me from the floor where I might have been trampled to death. With his arm around me, he led me out to safety. And we kept walking away, the nervous energy took over my body and I was so frightened. When we finally reached the large oak tree in the back by the stables, I couldn't breathe. But his face, he smiled at me with his hair tousled, his costume ruined. He reached out to touch my cheek. And I—," she paused, licking her lips as though the memory took her right back to that moment. "I stepped forward and kissed him."

Elizabeth blew out the breath she had held during her sister's recounting of the night that changed their lives forever.

"Did anyone see you?"

"I don't believe so. We feared gossip, that is why he stayed away initially, but there has been none," Jane said.

Closing her eyes, Elizabeth could see a face in her mind's eye that made her feel the emotions and stirrings similar to her sister's description: Mr. Darcy. Turning in her seat, she inspected her sister's face for sincerity. "What did it feel like?"

But Jane tucked her lower lip under her top one and shook her head. "Mmmhmmm, I shouldn't tell you, Lizzy. It was wicked of me to do it, and I am lucky that right after that Mr. Bingley proposed. He asked me to marry him."

"But Jane, that is so romantic! You know he loves you, truly, he risked his life to save yours!"

Jane raised an eyebrow at her sister. "Mr. Darcy did far more to save you," she pointed out, but Elizabeth crossed her arms in front of her chest. She kicked the front of the jockey box Mr. Bennet had added to the simple farm wagon to make it safer for his daughter's use.

"He's promised to another."

"I am not so sure. Mr. Bingley has never mentioned it. Our cousin is perhaps unreliable. He may have misunderstood. Have you asked Mr. Darcy about it?"

Elizabeth looked around, no longer worried about the duck under the wagon. "Where is William? Why has he not returned?" Elizabeth lifted the reins of the wagon to Jane's protestations. But Elizabeth glared at her sister. "I can't leave the wagon, remember? I will just drive us up to the lane around the cottage to the back, see, the ground is firm enough," Elizabeth said, and for a few moments, the plan worked splendidly. A loud quacking behind them attracted the notice of both young women, and they laughed to see the duck perfectly unharmed, but angry to lose his shaded respite.

Driving around the cottage to the farm yard, Elizabeth and Jane spied what held young William up for so long. The Widow Moran spoke animatedly with Mr. Bingley, who had dismounted from his horse, and Mr. Darcy behind him, still mounted. Mr. Bingley brightened upon spotting Jane and he waved. Elizabeth pulled the reins to bring the wagon to a halt, about ten yards from the congregation. Poor William stood dumbly holding the basket, unsure of what to do.

"Miss Bennet! What a surprise," Mr. Bingley said and walked forward to help Jane down from the wagon. He appeared confused for a moment, gazing back at William. "Oh! He's one of your family's men! But, this farm is on the lands of Netherfield."

"It is not!" Elizabeth shouted, scrambling to

exit the wagon herself. Mr. Darcy rode up on his horse, and then dismounted when he saw Elizabeth attempting to jump down. But by the time he reached her, she was already walking with a shaky gait to where Jane and Mr. Bingley stood. Mrs. Moran continued her diatribe about all of the problems with the property, from the leaky roof, to the improper drainage on the southern field.

"But now that you are here, Mr. Bingley, you can put a widow's mind at ease. My James here is a good lad. A strong lad. But always much more suited for books, not barns," she pointed in a direction utterly devoid of people. "See what I mean? Gone again! I'll catch him later doing sums."

Mr. Darcy furrowed his brow as he cleared his throat to speak. "I do beg your pardon, Miss Elizabeth, but we consulted the property lines this morning before our ride. This farm and two others further to the west are the last for us to inspect."

"How fortunate—" Elizabeth said, giving her sister a glare. She suspected that Jane had told Mr. Bingley of their plans last night at dinner, and this just cemented her suspicion that it was planned for them to happen upon Mr. Bingley and Mr. Darcy. "How fortunate we ran into you so that we can help correct the errors of your information. My Grandfather Bennet and Mr. Turner, who bought the property almost a hundred years ago, disputed that line for decades. My father and his counterpart, Mr. Turner's son, decided further legal action unnecessary. The line follows an ancient stream dried up from damming, and goes through fields and cottages on all three properties."

"The line is in dispute?" Mr. Darcy asked, to clarify, turning to look away from the group for signs of the water Miss Elizabeth talked about. But the ground showed no signs of depression or mounding from a cut of water swatching through. "I believe we have discovered why this property was vacant a leaseholder."

Elizabeth Bennet ignored Mr. Darcy and turned to Mrs. Moran. She urged William to present her with the basket. "I will have Mr. Harper come meet with you again, Mrs. Moran. He will go over all of the corrections the men will make in spring and my father will look for more hired help for the farm."

"But Mr. Bingley here was just saying how in situations like mine, the manor often gives a small token of appreciation and me and James could be moving to London. You'll make your coin bringing in a much larger family than mine, and when Mr. Moran was alive, I saw it for myself. There was never much left at the end of the season after paying out the hired help as you call it, and paying our rents each quarter."

Elizabeth closed her eyes and knew her father and Mr. Harper were going to be very cross about this morning. Somehow, it would become her fault for meddling again, she was the one who had sent books and ink for young James to learn his letters and sums. She had even sat with him a few times to give instruction, in the meadow with a few other children nearby since the church was too far for most of them to take their lessons regularly there.

"Well then, now that Mr. Bingley is here, and I believe here to stay for some time," Elizabeth said, putting words in the mouth of the man who had stirred the pot brewing with trouble, "he can help see that your wishes are met. But this is a conversation best saved for my father's man, and perhaps my uncle and Mr. Bingley," she said, with a finality, leaving Mr. Darcy out entirely. She begged Mrs. Moran's forgiveness that her injuries were bothering her and received the woman's sympathies.

"We all prayed hard, Miss Elizabeth, that you'd be well. I knew God could not take such a bright young lady from us so soon."

Elizabeth thanked her for the sentiment, and swallowed the bitter mouthful of bile that retched up into her mouth. Everyone kept telling her how protected she was, or how lovely it was that she survived. And each time she heard it, all she could think is what did that mean for those who perished? Aunt Phillips? Charlotte? Maria?

She waved over to William for his assistance to help her back to the wagon, much as it hurt her pride. When she had jumped down and walked quickly, she had forgotten that although her burns were mostly healed, she had not done any physical activity for two weeks. Her skin was also tight and uncomfortably itchy inside of her boots, and she was thankful her father wasn't present to see her indignity. He would have laughed at her expense and reminded her that she was to stay in the wagon.

Mr. Bingley and Jane spoked to Mrs. Moran for a moment longer, and then separated so that Mr. Bingley could mount his horse after helping Jane get back into the wagon. The new arrangement put Elizabeth in the middle of the jockey-box, which suited her just fine. Just as she predicted, the two gentlemen rode their horses at a slackened trot to escort the wagon to the last two houses. But before they left, Mr. Darcy spoke.

"Should we escort you back to Longbourn? If you have injured yourself, you should rest," he cautioned.

Elizabeth laughed. "Drive on, there's only two houses left. Besides, I had to say something to get us to move on or we'd be here until nightfall!"

The party of five continued their westward trek along the road that eventually led to another farm.

At the first one, William took the basket and Jane and Mr. Bingley escorted him as Mr. Bingley now wished to meet the neighbors he shared with the Bennets. Mr. Darcy remained on his horse, on the public road with Elizabeth.

"How did the Turners and your father mitigate the lack of a clear property line?" Mr. Darcy asked.

Elizabeth remained in the middle of the bench in the front of the wagon and groaned in annoyance. She remembered Jane's advice, but didn't think of any way to ask him if he was engaged to another without practically declaring her affection and interest in him. And if he was betrothed to another, she reasoned, her feelings for him were entirely inappropriate and might burden him unduly when he had already done so much for her.

Unlike Jane, she could not declare herself so openly and hope for it to be returned, she had thought herself in love before and it passed. Better to remain silent and wait, after all Jane would marry Mr. Bingley, she would always have a home.

Twisting in her seat, Elizabeth summoned happiness to conceal her turmoil by taking stock that she was outdoors and away from Mr. Collins. She chose to address Mr. Darcy with her feelings pushed aside and nothing but respect for the man's actions and words, as she knew them.

"They made an informal agreement to split the rent and responsibility. Our family traces back over five hundred years, our deeds are older than the surveyor who came through here in the early 1700s."

Mr.Darcy's horse showed frustration at having to hold still for so long, but Mr. Darcy kept the animal under control. As he spoke with a terse voice, Elizabeth observed that perhaps the beast merely reflected the mood of his owner. "But that is preposterous. Surely the surveyor took into consideration the existing property lines," he said.

Elizabeth laughed as this part of the story she knew well. "My ancestors were miserly, having lived through the uncertain century, as my father put it. A time when who could know where the crown would land? And so my father's great-grandfather refused the man lodging."

"He refused . . ."

"Yes," Elizabeth said, giggling. "Two generations of bickering over a bed and trench of stew!" she said, recalling how funny were all of the threatening letters. Once, an armed skirmish had occurred over three small farms. "In the end, my father, who hates conflict if you cannot surmise, and Admiral Turner, the son who never expected to inherit, decided they could both line their pockets if they came to an accord."

"But now the Admiral is dead," Mr. Darcy said, recalling the story he knew from Mr. Phillips when the lease was signed. "And the son and his mother wish to live in Town."

Elizabeth nodded.

"You seem to know far more than your sister, in matters of your family's estate."

Elizabeth blanched at his words, unsure if she should take them to be a compliment or condemnation. "My father relies upon me," she ventured.

"Yes, I can see that he does," Mr. Darcy said, as

the rest of the party returned. Calling Mr. Bingley over, the two men spoke briefly, and then Mr. Darcy nodded to both ladies and took off on his horse.

Jane became concerned for a moment and she inquired about Mr. Darcy leaving.

"Oh, he has some business to see to in Meryton. I assured him we could travel to the next farm ourselves," Mr. Bingley said, without taking his eyes off Jane. "And then, if I may, I should be happy to escort you ladies back to Longbourn."

Jane agreed with Mr. Bingley's plans, and the two of them carried the basket in themselves so that Elizabeth did not sit alone. As she watched the happy couple greet the Jones family, relations to the apothecary in the village, she felt as though she glimpsed her sister's future. When Jane and Mr. Bingley married, if he purchased Netherfield Park, then these families would continue to be taken care of for another generation. There would not be the acrimony and lack of respect that festered in their parents' marriage; Mr. Bingley sought Jane's opinion on everything it seemed.

Sighing that her sister was so fortunate to meet a man like Mr. Bingley, Elizabeth leaned forward and rested her chin in her hands.

"Pardon me, Miss Lizzy, but is there any cider

left?" William asked, and she handed the jug to him.

"Of course, Jane hardly touched her share," she said, offering the stable hand a means to quench his thirst.

The last stop ended up being the quickest as the prospect of returning to Longbourn satisfied everyone, including the horses. True to form, as soon as the two nags realized they had turned around, poor William struggled to keep them at a steady pace.

"Franny is always quick to rush back to the stables," Jane said, pointing to the bay dun horse forcing the pace on the older horse, Harvey.

Elizabeth stifled a yawn. "She knows there will be oats waiting for her. Never turns down a good meal," she replied drolly, just to make conversation. The horse's behavior provided her father an additional laugh when Elizabeth rode with him to inspect the farms. He would always jibe her and point out the similarities to the beast's namesake. Oh, Franny the horse loved to get out and socialize, and then ate more than any other horse in the stable.

Taking one last look at Mr. Bingley who elected to ride behind the wagon, Elizabeth smiled and then returned to looking forward to see the smoke rising in the distance from the manor house. She would demand that Mr. Bingley make her one promise when he married Jane, or perhaps more than one once she reconsidered, but at least this one: that he would never name a farm horse after Jane.

CHAPTER 12

If Elizabeth thought she would find respite at home, she was sadly mistaken. Instead of the leisurely, buffet style meal her family often enjoyed in the afternoon, not sitting down all together as her father rarely left his study on days he did not have to be out on the estate somewhere, their mother planned an altogether formal affair.

"Girls, you are returned. See Mr. Collins, I told you they would not be long," Mrs. Bennet said, greeting her eldest daughters, then upon spying Mr. Bingley, her voice hitched another half octave higher in tone. "And Mr. Bingley! What a pleasant surprise, sir, may I trouble you to stay for luncheon?"

Elizabeth blushed at her mother's assumption that Mr. Bingley would wish to eat with the women. Mr. Collins was one thing, the man was their cousin and staying in the home. But to invite Mr. Bingley simply showed how uncouth and unsophisticated she was.

"Thank you, very much, but is Mr. Bennet in? I should very much like an interview with him, if it pleases you. We traveled the farms, and I," he said, looking down at the mud and dirt from the morning's work that marred his boots and breeches, "I believe I should do better off with him."

Mrs. Bennet suddenly looked at her daughters and realized they too, looked a fright.

"Yes, certainly, I shall send a tray and ale to his study."

As Mr. Bingley reached down to formally kiss Jane's hand, Mrs. Bennet's eyes widened. He offered his signature lop-sided grin and then walked down the great hall to the study that was tucked so unobtrusively away on the first floor.

"Mama, taking the baskets to the tenants has fatigued me," Elizabeth began, trying to say she was too tired to eat downstairs. It was not even a lie, her body ached with pain and she desperately wanted to sleep.

"You may go upstairs to freshen yourself, and you, too, Jane dear, but then I expect you to come back down and eat in the dining room. Your days of being waited on hand-and-foot are over, Miss Lizzy. Did you really not think about how poor Mr. Collins might feel at being excluded this morning from your activity?" Mrs. Bennet scolded.

"But why should he have delivered baskets to tenants?" Elizabeth asked, pausing in her goal of reaching her room above stairs.

Mrs. Bennet swished her skirts with her hands, bristling at her daughter's stupidity.

"He is to *inherit*, and you could do very well for yourself if you would simply pay attention. I swear, your Father talks so much about your wits, but sometimes I don't understand what passes through that head of yours!" she exclaimed, turning away to plaster a false smile on her face and see about sending a tray to her husband's study.

Jane placed a comforting hand on Elizabeth's arm. "She worries for you, she believes that Mr. Bingley and I will marry, and it is a great honor, Lizzy, that she believes you might one day replace her."

Elizabeth's mouth melted into a frown

matching the rest of her expression of abject horror and disgust. "Me? Marry Mr. Collins?" she whispered, hoarsely. "There is no home in all of Britain that I could love so much as to tolerate that man's appalling manners and poor hygiene for all of eternity."

Believing the subject matter closed, Jane hurried them in complying with their mother's wishes. For a few moments, Elizabeth considered defying her mother's commands, but with her new freedom from her convalescence, she did not wish to curry her mother's interest in making her suffer.

At twenty years of age, gone were the days where she might be restricted to the house or her rooms for disobedience. But that didn't mean that her mother could not find other ways to make her displeasure known, namely by hounding Elizabeth with constant companionship and a never-ceasing vitriol of her thoughts on every matter. Even she was catching herself falling into the ways of her father: the best way to deal with Mrs. Bennet's desires and passions that conflicted with her own was to humor the woman until her interest in the matter waned or found a new employment.

By the time Jane and Elizabeth reached the dining room, their younger sisters had all been excused for finishing their meal.

"Jane, dear, do sit by me," their mother instructed so that Elizabeth was forced, once again, to sit next to Mr. Collins. But Elizabeth decided to use her wits that her mother had earlier insulted. She sat next to Jane, earning a look of disapproval from her mother.

"Are you settling in well, Mr. Collins?" Jane asked their guest, in an attempt to smooth over the palpable discomfort in the room.

"Very well! The room I have been appointed holds a lovely view of the pond and the stables. I noticed that Mr. Bingley escorted your wagon back, but did not see his friend, Mr. Darcy," Mr. Collins stated.

Elizabeth sliced a piece of cheese to go with her bite of cold meat. "He wished to make purchases in the village," she explained, flatly.

"Ah, gifts I'm sure for his sister, and perhaps Miss de Bourgh," Mr. Collins speculated, earning a nodding approval from Mrs. Bennet.

Elizabeth gagged at the mere mention of the woman Mr. Darcy was supposedly betrothed to marry. Hearing Mr. Collins speak so openly about the arrangement, she could not agree with Jane's assessment that believed the good in every one. Fighting back tears of anger, everything suddenly fell into place.

Mr. Darcy could not worry about being forced to marry her, a lowly squire's daughter, when he was already promised to another. Not that their father held any advantage over Mr. Darcy to compel him to take such steps. The man was good and kind in a way the Church instructed all men and women of nobler birth to be, just so few lived up to the charge.

Closing her eyes lest she begin to bawl, Elizabeth told herself over and over again that Mr. Darcy was a good man for all that he had done. This way, she silenced the voice in her mind that blamed him, unequivocally, for her new pain of a broken heart.

Mrs. Bennet, spying Elizabeth closing her eyes and worried her daughter might make another attempt at swooning, prodded Mr. Collins along.

"What were you telling me about Lady Catherine just a few moments ago?"

Mr. Collins appeared perplexed as he had been fascinated by staring at his Cousin Elizabeth to no avail. As much as he had liked the beauty of the eldest Bennet daughter upon entering the home, he could never say that the spirit and vivaciousness of the next in age was not beguiling. In his opinion, Elizabeth Bennet was more lovely and lively than he had ever hoped to make in a match.

"I beg your pardon, Mrs. Bennet. I cannot recall," he said, earning a small giggle from Cousin Jane, who elbowed her sister next to her. Mr. Collins frowned. Indeed, perhaps he had been lucky to arrive when he had, the eldest Bennet daughter was quite forward in her interactions with Mr. Bingley and while she appeared sweet and kind, her underhanded disrespect of him was something he could never abide.

Mrs. Bennet spoke louder as though that would help his recollection. "About how long you can visit us this time?"

Suddenly, Mr. Collins understood what he was meant to convey. "I have enjoyed speaking to your mother, Cousin Elizabeth, and I hope you will forgive my forwardness, but as my patroness, Lady Catherine de Bourgh advised me to spend not greater than a fortnight from my flock, I had thought to expand on my declaration last night. I believe that . . ."

Elizabeth had ceased to listen to the parson and elbowed her sister back, annoyed she had interrupted her daydreaming. But when Elizabeth angrily glared at her sister next to her, Jane's mouth hanging open in a stupor gave Elizabeth her first clue that something dreadful was transpiring.

"Almost as soon as I entered the house I singled you out as the companion of my future life. But before I am run away with my feelings on the subject, perhaps it will be advisable for me to state my reasons for marrying—and moreover for coming into Hertfordshire with a design of selecting a wife, as I certainly did."

"Jane," Elizabeth whispered, but Mr. Collins continued, undeterred.

"My reasons for marrying are, first, that I think it's a right thing for every clergyman in easy circumstances (like myself) to set the example of matrimony in his parish. Secondly, I am convinced it will add very greatly to my happiness; and thirdly—which perhaps I ought to have mentioned earlier, that it is the particular advice and recommendation of the very noble lady whom I have the honor of calling patroness. Twice as she condescended to give me her opinion, (unasked too!) on the subject; and it was but the very Saturday night before I left Hunsford, between our pools at quadrille, while Mrs. Jenkinson was arranging Miss De Bourgh's foot-stool—"

Elizabeth cringed as she could not believe what was happening. Somewhere in this diatribe, her cousin was going to ask her to marry him. And even if she didn't object on the many other grounds she reasonably held, such as his lack of physical or gentlemanly merits, or that she did not know the man at all despite his connection to her family, there was no possible way she could marry him. He would never consent to living at Longbourn until her father died, and she certainly could never show her face to this Lady Catherine de Bourgh and her daughter, feeling as she did about their relation and intended, Mr. Darcy.

"And now nothing remains for me but to assure you in the most animated language of the violence of my affection. To fortune I am perfectly indifferent, and shall make no demand of that nature on your father, since I am well aware that it could not be complied with—"

"You forget yourself, sir, I have given no answer," Elizabeth said, seething, wondering if this was what her father had spoken to Mr.

Collins about the previous night, her lack of dowry? Had he laughed when Collins squirmed, learning he would receive nothing to take a daughter off Mr. Bennet's hands? And thinking about the morning, had her father designed for her to tour the farms, in hope that she would feel nostalgia or some kind of affinity for the land she had grown up on, tended to, and loved?

"Lizzy, do not be hasty," her mother warned, earning a flash of her daughter's angry gaze, before she turned back directly to Mr. Collins.

Elizabeth pushed her chair back with little effort, fueled by the wrath of being manipulated by all. "I am very sensible to the honor of his proposal, but it is impossible for me to do otherwise than decline it."

She started to walk away, but her mother grasped her arm.

"Patience, Mr. Collins, this is a usual antic of a young lady overcome by such an overture," she tried to say as Elizabeth wrestled with her mother's grip.

Mr. Collins nodded. "Yes, I have heard that some ladies reject the addresses of the man they secretly mean to accept, when he first applies for their favor as means to test the earnestness of their suitor in making such an address again."

Finally free of her mother, Elizabeth stood out of her reach by the door, practically shouting.

"I am not one of those ladies! I am perfectly serious in my refusal. You could not make me happy, and I am convinced I am the last woman in the world who would make you so. Nay, were your friend Lady Catherine to know me, I am persuaded she would find me in every respect ill qualified for the situation!" she finished, finally allowing the tears over the loss of Mr. Darcy to flow freely.

Elizabeth ran out of the dining room just as the raised voices attracted the notice of Mr. Bingley and her father. They entered the dining room and her mother dived into hysterics.

"Mr. Bennet! Lizzy does not know her own interest! For she vows she will not have him," she said, pointing at the embarrassed Mr. Collins, "and if you do not make haste he will change his mind and not have her."

Mr. Bennet watched his daughter disappear and found himself mildly amused.

"Is this true, sir? You have proposed marriage to one of my daughters, professing to be affected and in love with her, but now find your resolve waning?" he asked, placing the burden of steadfastness upon the male suitor in question.

Mr. Collins stumbled over his words as Mr. Bingley walked carefully around Mrs. Bennet to stand near to Jane. "She refused me, sir. I was plain spoken and honest of my feelings and beliefs about why I thought we would suit. She disagrees, and showed a hasty temper I might also add, that if this is a common defect of hers, I agree with her that she could not contribute much to my felicity."

"Lizzy is only headstrong in such matters as these. In everything else she is a good-natured girl as ever lived," Mrs. Bennet tried to placate Mr. Collins.

"Ha!" Mr. Bennet scoffed, tucking his hands behind his back. He began to walk out of the dining room, but his wife gave him chase, catching him in the vestibule.

"Mr. Bennet you must make Lizzy marry Mr. Collins! Tell her you insist upon her marrying him!" Mrs. Bennet said, pointing at their daughter who returned with her cloak affixed around her shoulders and another degradation in her hands, a walking cane.

"Tell her!" Mrs. Bennet begged.

Mr. Bennet raised an eyebrow at his grown daughter, dressed for another adventure outdoors. He had seen Elizabeth angry enough times to know she struggled with a temper not unlike her mother's, only she sought control over the outbursts through activity.

"Where do you plan to go, my daughter?"

Elizabeth refused to meet his eye. "To see Father Graham."

Mr. Bennet turned to his wife. "See, my dear, you drive our second eldest to seek a nunnery, are you yet satisfied?"

Mrs. Bennet fumed as her husband angered her. He approached Elizabeth and gave a small peck upon her cheek. "I shall send the carriage to collect you in an hour's time," he offered.

Elizabeth nodded and left the chaos and confusion of her home behind. The temperature had begun a turn for the cold, with the wind whipping up to occasional blusters. But she didn't mind. She could not trek to her usual haunt up on Oakham Mount, but visiting the local parish, that lay just one mile away on the outskirts of Meryton, was a suitable distance for her to walk.

She stabbed the ground with ferocity in each step with her walking cane, understanding now why gentlemen made them an accessory of fashion. Believing her future to be a spinster old auntie, likely in Jane's household, or perhaps with her mother Heaven forbid, she chuckled at the idea of adopting the use of one at the earliest age possible. Canes were a perfectly adequate, comforting object when one needed to stew on one's feelings.

CHAPTER 13

Returning from Meryton with his purchases made, Mr. Darcy slowed his horse as he approached the churchyard. The unassuming stone chapel stood at a distance down the lane from the village proper, a path he selected. Another road would have taken him directly to Netherfield Park. But the road chosen, while longer, would take him past Longbourn, where his heart resided.

The church bell hung high in the tower, a prominent feature over the double wooden doors. Beside the sanctuary, a gathering of tombstones dotted the field leading back to the woods. A lone figure stood hooded in the yard, but he recognized the dark green cloak belonging to Miss

Elizabeth that he had just spied that morning. Guiding his steed to the gravel drive before the church, he dismounted and walked slowly, reverently to the woman he wished to count as his own.

When she did not turn despite his effort to make his presence known, he stood quietly behind her, willing her to feel well and happy. Before them were many stones darkened by age, the last names barely perceptible. And between the groupings, indentations of newly disturbed earth. The victims from the fire, all laid to rest two weeks ago but long before Miss Elizabeth had healed.

The tip of his nose began to grow cold and Darcy pulled his arms across his chest to keep his body heat close to him.

She shivered.

Feeling concerned, he stepped closer than propriety allowed, suddenly feeling another's gaze upon them. Turning around, the shadowy figure of the vicar stood in the window, almost like a ghostly apparition in the dim light. Mr. Darcy gulped, realizing that Elizabeth must have come to talk to him.

"Are you always so silent?" she asked, angrily.

Mr. Darcy abandoned his vigil of the church window to tend to the woman who had occupied his thoughts, sleeping and awake. He cleared his throat but felt a lump seize his airway.

"Well?" she demanded, turning around to face him, practically landing in his arms as she struggled to keep her balance with her walking cane.

Instinctively, he reached out to catch her at the elbow, steadying her stance. He gasped as tears streamed down her face.

"It is my experience that when young women cry, it is best to let their tears fall. Speak nothing and your words cannot worsen her affliction."

Elizabeth fumed at such a logical explanation that did nothing for her current predicament.

"Speak nothing and your words cannot soothe her affliction, either."

Mr. Darcy licked his lips and held his breath. She was so close to him and yet the distance between them felt great.

"You are far from home," he remarked, looking north in the direction of Longbourn. "Should you be walking this far when you've only recently recovered?" he asked, looking down at the walking stick that belied her true condition since the fire.

"I walk better than they do," she said, sniffing, and regaining her composure.

"I am most pained for your loss. That night was . . ." he trailed off, catching her gaze. Locking eyes with her flooded his mind with memories of the assembly before the great tragedy.

"Many lost more. I loved my dear friend, but she was not my sister, my daughter," Elizabeth said, reminding herself of how she must not fall too deeply into a melancholy that was not her burden. Those were the reassuring words of the vicar, though Elizabeth had wanted more answers than that. Charlotte and Maria were both so young, why had John not been able to find them? She would never wish her sisters had not been spared, but how had the Bennets been so lucky and the Lucases not?

Mr. Darcy offered his arm to provide an opportunity to walk. Elizabeth shifted her walking stick to her left hand and looped her right through his. Unconsciously, he led her over to the bench on the far side of the churchyard. But she refused to sit down when they reached it.

"Part of me wishes you had left me in the tavern," she said, quietly.

The words made him halt.

"You cannot mean that."

Elizabeth turned towards him with a defiant stare. "What is it like to live your life purely by your own desires and wants?"

Confused, Mr. Darcy replied with a shorter tone than he intended. "I cannot guess, I have never lived in such a manner."

"At least your family places no demands upon you." She snorted as she acridly thought once more about her buffoon of a cousin, encouraged and manipulated by her parents, offering a proposal of marriage on the second day of their acquaintance.

"I have no mother or father, but I assure you that guardianship of my sister has not granted me a light responsibility."

Elizabeth thought for a moment, Dr. Stevens had mentioned that Mr. Darcy had a sister. "But you travel without her. Who is she with when you are gone?"

Mr. Darcy gritted his teeth, suddenly feeling accused of some great crime he did not believe Miss Bennet could possibly have any information about. "It is for her protection! Not every young lady strives to live so wholly independent of everyone around her."

Elizabeth smirked. “A fault of mine you surely disapprove."

Mr. Darcy caught the twitch of a smile on her lips and realized he had been goaded into a fallacy of logic. He could not suddenly claim to disapprove of Elizabeth's headstrong and independent ways when he had so often enjoyed the opportunity to know her better.

"I would approve most ardently of a lady who served her needs, and the needs of others, as circumstances dictated."

"And her desires?" she whispered.

He granted her a roguish smile, making her giggle and blush.

"If only I am so fortunate enough to make them my concern."

Stunned by his forwardness, Elizabeth finally took a seat on the cold bench to remind herself of her circumstances. Her attraction to Mr. Darcy was nothing she could deny, but it did not follow that the man was anything more than an incorrigible flirt! He was promised to another!

“Forgive me, I have offended you,” he said, taking a seat next to her.

Elizabeth chose to change the subject to Jane. She knew not why, but her heart felt that if she brought up Mr. Bingley and her sister, she could perhaps deduce an answer about Mr. Darcy's behavior.

"My sister disclosed to me what passed between her and your friend. Were you aware they have been secretly engaged since the night of the fire?" she asked.

"I held suspicions and Bingley confirmed more to me this morning. But I believe last night your father approved of a respectful courtship, in light of your family's loss."

"Indeed, there will be two felicitous unions, although I am unsure when the other shall take place."

Mr. Darcy closed his eyes and suspected the worst. "Your cousin, then, he brought the matter to a point?"

"He did," she sniffed.

"I suppose I should wish you joy," he spat, rising from the bench, believing she had accepted her cousin out of duty to her family and therefore the source of her tears. Elizabeth watched him curiously as the man appeared suddenly greatly agitated. Then he turned around, and his eyes were pained again.

"But it is not too late if I were to step forward and speak to your father?"

"There is nothing you could say to my father

to change your circumstances, sir. And why would you wish me joy?"

Mr. Darcy blinked. His mind raced. "Miss Elizabeth, are you engaged to marry your cousin?" he asked.

Elizabeth shook her head. "But you are engaged to your cousin, and it is I who should wish you joy, but I am afraid I cannot," she uttered, grinding the cane into the dirt to rise from the bench. She started to turn away but he grasped her free hand, then bowed solemnly over it, kissing the top.

"In vain have I struggled. It will not do. My feelings will not be repressed. You must allow me to tell you how ardently I admire and love you," he professed, breathlessly.

Elizabeth held her breath. She had considered perhaps he felt an attraction to her, but not that he loved her! Was she truly to entertain two proposals in one day?

"I was concerned at first, that my feelings were the product of the crisis, the fire, and the warnings of your father affirmed such, but I overcame that worry when you fell ill again. I realized what the Bard writes could be true, 'Hear my soul speak. Of the very instant that I saw you, Did my heart fly at your service.'"

Blushing, Elizabeth looked down, not trusting herself to speak at first. She tried to sort through her thoughts on the matter, now that he had declared. She wanted to tell him that at first she despised his vanity, but learned it was his protection of self against an uncomfortable situation.

She also wanted to tell him how she worried that because he had rescued her, there was a feeling of an impossible debt, one she could never hope to repay. Like him, she also could not trust her first feelings because they came mixed with so much pain and despair of the future, even a small glimmer of hope blazed brightly.

"And I very nearly offered for your hand last night, but then your mother laid bare the circumstances of your family—"

Anger suddenly returned to Elizabeth's consciousness. She was to endure two proposals in one day it appeared and both men took exception to her family's status.

"Mr. Collins I might rightly understand finding concern with my dowry, but those with so much can surely hold no scruples about such trifling matters?"

"Mr. Collins?" Mr. Darcy released her hand as her interruption derailed his confession about overcoming such obstacles to making an offer for her hand, which he had not entirely completed.

"Yes, Mr. Collins."

"You compare my declaration of love and admiration to his?"

Elizabeth defiantly glared at the man she so urgently wanted to kiss and at the same time, run away from. Thus far in her experience, Mr. Darcy achieved his aims. He answered to no one. His manners, though not entirely rude, often left little consideration for others when he was so quick to be direct.

"The man stated similar positions, though he did remark on singling me out, which I suppose he meant as a compliment. When he began to declare my lack of fortune concerned him not, I also cut him off just this afternoon."

Mr. Darcy opened his mouth to speak but faltered when it came to words.

No longer as affected by the physical attraction to Mr. Darcy now that she was no longer feeling his touch, Elizabeth allowed her mind to wander and realize the utter folly of her life.

"Did you also intend to profess your love for me amongst the graves?" she asked, so matter-of-factly, the spell of romance was thoroughly shattered.

"No," he replied.

"Well, thank goodness for that, I suppose," she said, making a silly face at him to dispel his anger as well, and the man laughed. He again offered her his arm, and she accepted, the physical activity needed to salve both of their wounded egos. This time, he began their walk back to the other side, where his horse waited for him.

"I cannot speak for other men, but I am not certain I shall recover swiftly from this rejection," he stated.

Elizabeth's tinkling laughter almost brought him to the brink of rage again.

"I did not reject you, sir. You asked me no question," she pointed out. There was no completion to his proposal any more than their last chess game. But this time, she did not grant him a chance to speak more and undo the small truce they held.

She stopped walking and turned to face him. Closing her eyes, she resolved to be brave, like her sister Jane.

"Please, before you ask me anything, I ask for time," she managed, finally opening her eyes to see his, suddenly not pained but bright and wide with happiness. "If you will permit, though I was not so kind in granting you full range to vent your concerns, I would like for you to hear mine."

Still stunned that she had declared he was not rejected, Mr. Darcy cleared his throat, glancing nonchalantly at the church window. As he suspected, the vicar stared from the window still.

"I would hear anything that you would tell me," he confessed.

Elizabeth took a deep breath and they began walking again. "I am not quite well from the fire. My feet are pained still, and I suffer nightmares."

"I should recall Dr. Stevens," he said, and she emphatically stated otherwise.

"That is part of my reservation. You did not listen to me when I expressed that I did not want my burns treated by him. Nor did my father listen, so I give you grace that you at least did not know me well enough. But that day, and my subsequent illness are worsened in memory because I held no control over my person," she stated, taking a moment to glance at his face and seeing he looked confused.

She sighed, then paused once more, placing both hands upon the cane she used to help her walk. "Men answer to themselves. Wives answer to their husbands. I would very much like to respect and esteem you beyond the trappings of a physical attraction, as I have seen the damage left behind when such passion fades."

"You fear I will stop loving you?" he asked.

Elizabeth smiled. "In a way, or perhaps come to love me in a way aberrant, as a means of preserving your peace."

Mr. Darcy tilted his head to the side as he considered what Elizabeth spoke, assuming she was describing the marriage her parents had.

"I also do not wish to lose my voice over my own life. I have seen my mother, desperate to fix problems she sees, problems which require the aid of my father. And he mocks her."

"I will never mock you," Mr. Darcy promised.

"I sincerely hope we never mock each other, tease gently, perhaps, but not the cruel, tormenting kind of dismissal that comes from derision, not devotion."

Mr. Darcy reached out for her hand, but she held fast to the cane.

"You have considered your future happiness a great deal, it seems," he observed, still holding out hope she would accept his offered gesture.

"That is why I ask for time. Time for us to

learn of each other, time for us to know one another, before we . . ." Her words trailed off as she could not quite bring herself to assume they would wed, practically proposing to him!

"And I shall honor your request, Elizabeth," he said, daring to use her first name as a means of cementing their unorthodox understanding.

"Thank you, Fitzwilliam," she tried, taking his hand and smiling.

Waiting by Mr. Darcy's horse, a conspicuous carriage sat parked and the happy couple made their way back to the church drive. Mr. Bingley and Jane descended from the carriage, eager to congratulate the couple, but both of them shook their heads at the exuberant expressions of their respective sister and friend.

Mr. Bingley's expression fell first, quite vexed at his friend's nonverbal communication of shaking his head. "But, but, you two appear as though—"

Elizabeth laughed. "Do not worry, Mr. Bingley. Mr. Darcy and I are still friends," she said, with a knowing smile to the gentleman next to her.

Spying no one else in the carriage, Elizabeth suddenly felt embarrassed anew by her own family. What was Jane thinking? What was her mother thinking sending Jane by herself?

"After you left, Lizzy, Mama was unbearable. Father left for the library and Mr. Collins sulked until deciding to take himself out for a walk. She was such a nervous wreck that I couldn't bear it any longer."

Elizabeth blushed and noticed Mr. Darcy kept to a stony expression of indifference. Her heart pained for him to be reminded of Mr. Collins' proposal and she almost wished she could take back her words that halted his own.

"So," Mr. Bingley built suspense, then reached down to take Jane's hand and kissed it. "We told her! That Mr. Bennet had agreed to courtship and now, thanks to Mrs. Bennet, there will be a wedding!"

"In the New Year," Jane gushed, receiving an embrace from her sister.

"That is wonderful news!" Elizabeth said, and realizing the sky was getting darker by the moment, regretfully reasoned that they ought to be leaving.

Elizabeth boarded the carriage with Jane and Mr. Bingley, and Mr. Darcy bowed and mounted his horse. To their surprise, he rode ahead and left the slow-moving vehicle behind.

Not a quarter-mile down the road, Jane began needling her sister, despite Mr. Bingley's presence.

"Whatever did you do to offend Mr. Darcy?" she asked.

Elizabeth shook her head. "Oh he is not offended, I believe. Driven perhaps, by a mission."

Mr. Bingley laughed as he sat next to Jane. "See, I told you we did not need to intervene where it came to those two."

Elizabeth raised an eyebrow at Mr. Bingley, eternally grateful it had indeed not come to any interference on his part.

"Is he engaged to his cousin?" Jane asked.

Elizabeth shook her head.

As she turned away from her sister to stare out the window, she communicated that she did not wish to speak any further on the subject. It was just as well because Jane and Mr. Bingley began discussing plans for the following day of his sister hosting the ladies for tea, plans that were not yet shared with Miss Bingley.

As elated as Elizabeth had felt in the previous hour, working out an understanding with Mr. Darcy in the odd manner they had managed, the joy evaporated to her more familiar companion of melancholy. She had not told a falsehood that there was more healing for her to do, in her body, mind, and spirit. With any luck, the wedding of Jane and Mr. Bingley would take the focus off of her for the next few weeks granting her that space to do so.

CHAPTER 14

Dinner at Longbourn reduced the table numbers to the Bennets and Mr. Collins. Despite Mrs. Bennet's wishes otherwise, Mr. Bingley was encouraged by the patriarch of the family to dine at home. After the day's tumultuous events in engagements, failed engagements, and near engagements, even Mr. Bingley had to agree the household needed peace.

Summoned to her father's study after the meal, Elizabeth hoped to play a game of chess or backgammon. Instead, she found her father sitting behind his desk. Feeling as though the discussion would be personal, she closed the door behind her. Her shoulders tensed as he said her name in a tone she knew meant he desired answers.

"I had the strangest visit from Mr. Darcy this afternoon, Child. He came to inform me that he would be leaving the neighborhood for some weeks but planned to return for Jane and Mr. Bingley's wedding after Christmas."

Elizabeth nodded as none of this was news to her. She had seen Mr. Darcy just after his interview with her father, where he told her much the same, promising he would return. She hadn't contradicted him but felt the decision hindered her desire to get to know him better.

"What passed between the two of you this afternoon?" her father asked.

Elizabeth shrugged her shoulders, earning a hollow laugh from Mr. Bennet.

"Oho, you as well? He also would not tell me much, though he did relay some," he said, raising an eyebrow but his daughter kept her face slackened without revealing more. "He begged of me two requests. One, I already granted, but the second . . ."

"Papa! What has Mr. Darcy asked of you?"

Mr. Bennet considered his daughter's earnest reaction. He had anticipated that buffoon Collins would never listen to him that to win over his Cousin Elizabeth, he would need to humble himself to impress her. Walking in as heir presumptive could never persuade her to make a match. Not his Lizzy. Of course, the man did not listen, instead employing the silly advice of his wife. Now, his favorite companion stood before him, clearly besotted by the stranger from Derbyshire, the same man who saved her life. And Mr. Bennet hated every moment of it.

"Sit, sit, here," he invited her to the chair beside his desk and to her surprise, offered her a pouring of brandy. She accepted the glass and raised it with her father for a sip, while he took a healthy swig. "Now, please do not insult my intelligence and claim nothing has passed between you. Whatever it is, I will hold the confidence. I never said a word about Jane," he pointed out.

Elizabeth ran her finger along the glass rim. The deep amber libation left a telling haze on the inside where she had sipped. "That is true, Mr. Bingley practically boasted that he is the one who disclosed their secret," she agreed with him.

Mr. Bennet raised his hand, palm flattened to emphasize his earlier point.

Still, something twisted in Elizabeth's gut that she did not feel comfortable telling her father all that had passed between her and Mr. Darcy. She also felt equally stupid to pretend nothing had happened between them. If he renewed his offer, she would have a very difficult time convincing her father of her regard.

"Mr. Darcy came upon me walking near Charlotte's grave," she began, and her father gasped. Whatever he had expected to be the story, it was clearly not to begin on such a dark note. "After we spoke for some time, he professed love and admiration, but I prevented him from coming to the point of asking for my hand."

His jaw fallen in awe, Mr. Bennet stared at his daughter in disbelief.

"Do you not like Mr. Darcy?" he asked.

Elizabeth scowled at her father, finding his behavior too simple-minded.

"I scarcely know Mr. Darcy," she stressed.

"Ah," he said, partaking of his drink and nodding his head. "Without prying further, assuming he did not assault you or otherwise molest you?" Mr. Bennet asked, half-teasing, but necessary details to know if they were true.

Elizabeth emphatically shook her head. "No, no, nothing of that kind. Mr. Darcy was the perfect gentleman."

"How did you end it with him?"

Elizabeth shrugged again and treated herself to more brandy. The sting on her tongue echoed as a singe up to her nose, but she enjoyed the warm burn down her esophagus. She smacked her lips at the tart aftertaste, making her father laugh. "I don't suppose you could say I ended it with him at all. I asked him to grant me time before renewing his addresses, if he ever does," she said, ending her summary with a slight sadness to her voice.

"I see, I see."

Mr. Bennet refilled his snifter but did not offer Elizabeth another drop. He swirled the topaz liquid in his glass, watching the trick of the candlelight and fire in the reflection.

"Papa, I have told you all that you have wished to know unless you'd like the details of how it felt when he touched my hand, and how my breath caught in my chest when he declared—"

"No, no, none of that!" he said, playfully covering his ears and humming a tune.

Elizabeth cackled at the easy time she had with her father and finished her brandy whilst he worked out keeping his end of the bargain. Quick footsteps trampled back and forth across the hall and they both looked at the door.

"Your sisters are terrible eavesdroppers," he commented, blandly.

"Nay," Elizabeth countered, and listened as a

distinct yelp and more footsteps could be heard. "Sounds like Lydia and Kitty are picking on one another, anything to avoid Mr. Collins reading in the parlor."

"Indeed, those two could never be quiet long enough to conceal their whereabouts." Mr. Bennet sighed, as he suddenly felt like a much older man than his forty-six years. Elizabeth looked at him expectantly and he decided he would not make her embarrass herself further by declaring more solid feelings for the man.

"In light of what you have shared, I am most proud of you for never giving in to fear, my Lizzy. Granted, you likely have known for some time that Jane will marry Mr. Bingley. Still, many other young ladies would have never dared to reject a man like Mr. Darcy."

"But I didn't reject him! I was quite clear, I asked only for time."

"Heh, perhaps retell that tale to Mr. Bingley's sister, that one who always puts on too much perfume," he described, wrinkling his nose. "I think she might declare you fit for Bedlam!"

Elizabeth pursed her lips, hoping her father would not traipse further down this path of speculation. How could she tell him the nightmares she confessed to Mr. Darcy were not always at night, but sometimes in the middle of the day? While she was awake, almost anytime she was alone?

"Father," she warned.

"Aside from the jewels and carriages you might have had, Lizzy, the man seems to have accepted your terms. I do believe he will be back. He gave this to me, allowing me to judge the best time to bestow it," Mr. Bennet said, reaching into the drawer of his desk, he pulled out a wooden box. "I believe with him leaving the area for a few weeks, now is as good a time as any,"

Elizabeth accepted the box, startled by its heftiness.

"He bought me a gift?" she asked.

"And gave it to me so that all was done properly," Mr. Bennet pointed out.

Considering the plain pine box for a moment, she could not discern any markings or indications as to what it might be. Using a knife from her father, she cut the twine holding the lid in place. Once she managed to pry it off, she gasped at the trove of treasures inside. A dozen glass jars with cork stoppers lay nestled in the box, in three neat rows, full of pigments in various colors. At the bottom of the box, two larger parcels of mediums lay sealed.

"He included beeswax," she said, giggling.

Mr. Bennet smiled. "Perhaps he doesn't know how much you've troubled our hives," he explained.

"But how did he know at all? I've never told him that I paint," Elizabeth said, suspiciously.

Mr. Bennet lifted a few of the jars and held them up to the light, squinting to see the color. But each one looked similar to another, just a jar of dust. A few, the dull yellow and the chalky white he could spy were different from the others. "While you were recovering from the fire before you woke up, the man spent most of the day and evening here. Truthfully, we both worried it was in vain what he had done, and I was only grateful he was not also seriously injured," Mr. Bennet recounted.

"He stayed here? I thought that was an embellishment when Lydia told me," Elizabeth said, thoughtfully. Suddenly, her familiar friend of guilt washed over her heart, fingering the expensive gift Mr. Darcy had bought, and knowing that the man had kept vigil. She had little right to ask him to wait at all, but then she scolded herself once more, that was precisely why she needed time. If she accepted him out of obligation, she could never give him the love he so plainly deserved.

"Yes, he mostly stayed in here. Pleasant fellow, to tell you the truth, not one looking to talk to fill the silence," Mr. Bennet described, and Elizabeth agreed. "He had inspected all of my books, read one or two, and one day commented on my miniatures," Mr. Bennet said, pointing to the work of his daughter.

"And you told him I was the painter," she finished.

"Well, I certainly couldn't lie to the man. I was proud. . . and concerned. We thought we might lose you, Lizzy," Mr. Bennet said, choking on his last words.

Elizabeth closed her eyes, feeling the prick of tears welling up in her tired eyes. She still had not rested since the morning hours and their trek out to the tenant farms. Her father placed a hand over hers, the touch comforted her and she opened her eyes allowing her tears to fall.

Softly, she apologized. "I am so sorry."

"Do not apologize for who you are, Lizzy. If Jane had been in there, you would have found her. You two have tumbled, tagged along, and followed one another on every adventure of your childhoods." He paused and chuckled to himself over his personal memories.

"But she was not. I only found Charlotte, and I could not save her."

Mr. Bennet wisely poured his daughter another small glass of brandy and did not refill his own.

"What did you find when you were in that inferno?" he asked, prompting Elizabeth to unburden herself.

"There was smoke, so much smoke."

He nodded. "Yes, Mr. Darcy covered his mouth, I hear, with a cloth before going in after you," Mr. Bennet explained.

Elizabeth didn't register her father's words. In her mind, the study was the assembly room, ablaze with a fire that scorched her skin and choked her breath. Her voice cracked and groaned as she told her father more. "I could not see, or breathe, and I fell to the floor. Charlotte was there, on the floor, her arm outstretched . . ." Elizabeth closed her eyes and reached out, miming the horror for her father.

Mr. Bennet gasped but held strong. With a clear voice, he asked his daughter a question that she needed to hear. "Was Charlotte alive? Was she moving?"

Elizabeth flinched as she tried to remember, and she shook her head hesitantly, then twitched and shook it more vigorously. She had reached out for Charlotte and pulled, pulled as hard as she could, and her friend hadn't moved.

"No," Elizabeth's voice shook with emotion. She opened her eyes and forced herself to match her father's gaze. "No," she repeated, then picked up the glass of brandy with her arm that had mimicked the stretch, and drank more of it. Two gulps and she finished the glass.

"There was nothing you could have done. It is a miracle you were spared."

"No, Papa, it was not a miracle," Elizabeth countered. "It was Mr. Darcy."

Agreeing to leave her gift in his study until the morning, Elizabeth yawned, feeling the effects of the brandy and exhaustion of the day. She had rarely felt so tired and worn out, but truly, she thought she might sleep for days again.

"I'll tell your mother not to disturb you in the morning," he promised, as Elizabeth finally stood to walk to the door.

She yawned once more before turning the latch. "What was the other request Mr. Darcy made?" she asked, sleepily, leaning against the wall to keep herself upon her feet.

Mr. Bennet chuckled. "Nothing gets past you, my Lizzy."

She grinned like a drunken cat and nodded.

"He asked if he could write to you, through me."

Elizabeth shivered with a sudden jolt of alertness. "And?" she implored.

"I heartily gave my consent," Mr. Bennet said, with a sage nod.

Rewarded with his daughter's happiness, Mr. Bennet wished her a good night's rest and tucked his bottle of brandy away. What little time they had known Mr. Darcy was filled with such assurances, if he had known another man thousands of times as long, Mr. Bennet doubted very much he'd know a man's character more thoroughly.

CHAPTER 15

The next morning, Elizabeth could not prevent herself from waking with the dawn. Pleasantly surprised and elated to feel more like her old self, she tested her body by closing her eyes once more to see if she could fall back asleep. She smiled when she could not, her body had completely replenished her energies. She relished finding herself again: the woman before the fire.

Jane's soft snoring in the bed next to her made her chuckle. While they both had endured the same lengthy previous day, Elizabeth cut her night short by hours compared to her sister. Since the revelation of Jane's engagement to Mr. Bingley, their mother began planning as though the event was scheduled for tomorrow. Instead, it was to be one week after Christmas.

After dressing for the day, Elizabeth began a search for the items she had worn to the assembly. Her gown she knew had been reduced to the rag pile. She hoped some of the trimmings were salvageable for the staff. The simple gold cross that she had worn since her sixteenth birthday had been safely recovered and rested against her collar bone. It was a silly notion, but she suddenly hoped the pale pink ribbon that she had worn in her hair survived her ordeal. Frantically, she searched the basket holding many of the ribbons that she and her sister Jane used regularly, but she did not find any trace of the pretty ribbon from that fateful night. Touching her curls, her mind felt washed in relief that her hair had not caught fire! She supposed if one had to succumb, much better it be the ribbon than her crowning glory.

Disappointed, she shoved the basket back onto the shelf and deflated to a kneeling position on the wooden floor to reconsider her aims. One of the messages from Father Graham, apart from avoiding deep positions of mourning not rightfully hers to claim, included the encouragement of gratitude. His advice to her grief was to find ways and means of giving to those around her. From her lowered vantage point, she spotted her old sketchbooks from the last few years neatly tucked in a row. Reverently, her fingers traced their spines and she selected one that she was fairly confident might hold the images she desired.

The first few pages contained the failed efforts every artist created under the pressure of a new leather bound book. Too much opportunity and optimism. As much as she wished for every sketch to be perfect in every way, the trappings of her abilities not meeting her expectations humbled her again and again. Callously, she turned the pages quickly to move past the offending efforts. Falling to a page displaying the outside of Lucas Lodge, she grinned. She turned a few more pages and eventually she was rewarded with precisely what she was looking for: a number of sketches of Charlotte and Maria from last spring when they consented to pose for her during a lovely picnic.

Satisfied with what she had found, she dusted off her skirts and carefully placed the sketchbook on her writing desk near the window. Between her memories and the references in her sketchbook, she would be able to put Mr. Darcy's most generous gift to good use. She would create a painting with the spring motif for Sir William Lucas and his lady as a small way of appeasing her guilt of surviving when their daughters had not. Spying the sun's light gaining an edge against the dark night, Elizabeth began to fret once more.

Hastily, she plucked her cloak off the peg and fastened it around her shoulders. She donned her boots and found the infernal walking stick, but stood paralyzed a moment and returned to her earlier dilemma. She started the whole morning wishing to thank Mr. Darcy for his gift of pigments, but dared not write him a letter. It might be a fool's errand entirely, as she hinged her efforts on catching his carriage as he took his leave of the county. But something told her he would direct his carriage past Longbourn, even if it was in the opposite direction of his travels.

As Jane muttered in her sleep, Elizabeth realized a ribbon from the night of the fire wasn't necessary at all! She dashed over to the vanity and found the longer yardage of ribbon that she had cut the night of the assembly for her hair piece. Using shears, she trimmed another piece, this one only a few inches long. She grinned at the idea of offering Mr. Darcy her "token," a piece of nondescript ribbon that's only significance would be known between her and him. As she held the pale pink ribbon up to her face in the looking glass, she spied the haunting visage of Charlotte for a moment. Quickly, Elizabeth blinked and looked behind her, but it was just the reflection of Jane sleeping. Still feeling unsettled, she tucked the ribbon into the pocket of her gown and hoped that Mr. Darcy would understand her gift was more sentiment than function.

When she at last left through the kitchens, where the staff had once more prepared the daily breakfast for the adventurous Bennet daughter and placed it in a handkerchief, Elizabeth felt utterly restored in a way she felt she did not deserve. She used the walking cane to maintain her steady pace down the drive to where the main road connected to her father's property. She could not have planned her timing better because down the road about half a mile, she could plainly see the arrival of a carriage. She wondered, as she watched the approaching conveyance, what Mr. Darcy would have done if she had not taken the initiative to meet him? Would he have held the carriage in case she appeared? Turned into the drive and come to the house properly to say farewell to her father?

As the vehicle came to a slower pace to minimize the dust, she decided upon the last possibility. Realizing she might startle Mr. Darcy by being at the end of her father's drive, she began to laugh just as the door opened and the gentleman revealed himself.

"Miss Elizabeth!" he exclaimed, holding himself from greeting her too familiarly, and offering a low bow.

"Mr. Darcy," she replied, offering him a curtsy. "Would you like to take a small walk around the drive with me before your long journey?" she brazenly asked, and the man happily agreed.

Once they were out of earshot of the driver and guard, Elizabeth began the conversation with her eternal gratitude for his thoughtful gift.

"I see that your father gave it to you before I even left the area," he said, sounding slightly disappointed.

"Oh, had you intended it to be a Christmas gift?" she asked, perplexed as she never could have accepted such a gift in front of her family, not when they were not engaged.

"No," he said, signaling he understood such a circumstance would have been impossible. "I only wished that he had waited until I was gone, you see, to perhaps remind you of my affections some time in the near future," he explained.

Elizabeth thought for a moment as more than once the man's statements baffled her understanding. A swift glance to his face and she understood the emotion he was trying to express: fear. He feared she might not hold any regard for him while he was gone.

"I admit I did wonder at you leaving the neighborhood," she said gently, not wishing to sound too cold.

Reaching into his great coat, Mr. Darcy pulled out a sealed piece of parchment. He pressed it to Elizabeth's hand and dumbly she accepted it without thought, sliding it into her gown pocket. The movement reminded her of her gift, and she allowed her fingers to find the slip of satin.

"I detailed part of my explanation. Of course, I have been away from my affairs for over a month, and I am traveling north to Pemberley for Christmas," he explained.

"Couldn't be tempted by Miss Bingley to stay at Netherfield, eh?" Elizabeth teased, relaxed in his presence to give him a grin that exposed her full smile. His eyes lit up at the sentiment offered.

"Err, no," he replied, lifting her hand to his lips, he kissed the top of her exposed hand as she had not thought to don gloves. "Your hands are so cold," he noticed, with a frown.

Elizabeth blushed as she suddenly realized she desired more than kisses upon her hand. Jane was correct, this kissing business was frightfully dangerous!

"I shouldn't keep you longer, but I shall return as soon as I am able," he said, bowing.

"Wait!" she exclaimed, fumbling to pull the ribbon out of her pocket with the letter, but she struggled.

Mr. Darcy paled, fearing she was returning the letter, but sighed with relief when her hand appeared in a closed fist, but clearly not with the missive.

"It is not the same as what I wore that night—" she said quickly, flustered and suddenly nervous. "That night," she repeated, "you saved me. But it is from the same spool and like you, I was hoping you might remember me while you are away," she whispered, holding her fist out. He stretched out his hand and when she opened hers, he didn't feel anything at first. But when she removed her hand, he could finally see the gift.

"Elizabeth," he uttered, in a voice of reverence. The ribbon was slightly crumpled, but holding it safely in one palm, he gently traced the length with his pointer finger on his other hand. "I shall keep it with me always."

Elizabeth giggled. "I appreciate the sentiment, but do not think I will believe your faithfulness waivers if there are times when carrying around a silly, little ribbon is not convenient."

"To others, yes, it appears to be an ordinary bit of ribbon. But to me, it is so much more," he said, arresting her attention with the strained passion in his voice.

Elizabeth allowed herself to fall helplessly enthralled by his expressive eyes, hoping her own reflected all of the words and emotions she dared not share. Not yet.

Again he bowed, and after tucking his treasure carefully away, he walked rigidly back to the carriage. Elizabeth watched his tall frame for a few moments, until she could hear the front door of Longbourn open behind her and the voices of her family drift out. Turning around and enjoying a sharp, satisfying grind of her walking stick into the ground, she returned to her sisters waiting in the doorway.

CHAPTER 16

"Was that Mr. Darcy?" Kitty asked, scrunching her nose up and looking down the lane. Elizabeth groaned as her sister dared to come outside with her paper curls still in her hair!

"Kitty!" she said, sternly, ushering her and Mary back into the house. "Why would you come outside in such a state?"

Kitty pouted. "It's hardly a respectable time to call," she countered, crossing her arms.

"Will Papa force you to marry Mr. Darcy?" Mary asked, solemnly.

Elizabeth rolled her eyes, reaching her hand into the pocket that contained the letter to keep it's sharp edges from poking out. "I am not compromised. I stood in clear sight of my father's home in broad daylight," she taunted.

Leaving her younger sisters to argue as Kitty was no longer happy that Mary had roused her so early from bed, Elizabeth sought the refuge of her room. Jane still slumbered and Elizabeth took advantage of the privacy to read her letter at her writing desk. Just to be safe, she removed a few letters from their aunt in London in case she was interrupted.

She inspected the front of the letter and noticed he had not addressed it to her. Slightly saddened to not see her name penned by his hand, she reasoned it was safer all the same in case the letter was intercepted. Turning it over, her fingers touched the seal's intaglio, the horns of a ram and antlers of a stag criss-crossed over a stylized letter F and D. She wondered if Mr. Darcy owned a signet ring for his mark like her father, or if he used a seal stamp like her uncle? Realizing she could one day learn the answer, she felt a flush of warmth spread over her, reminding her to hurry and read the letter before she was interrupted.

. . .

*B*E NOT ALARMED, *Madam, on receiving this letter. If your father has not already apprised you, though I wished to say something yesterday in our final interview but there were too many present, I have received permission for him to write to you. Future correspondence of course shall be addressed to him, but for this letter that I hoped to begin our path forward to a mutual happiness, I intend on delivering it to your hand. If you are reading this, then I have prevailed. Perhaps it is bold of me to appear confident you will accept my future addresses, as I have now heard tale you hold no compunction reminding a wayward suitor when you have not given an answer.*

Elizabeth scoffed at his gentle tease. Kitty and Mary's argument continued up the stairs, and she waited to see if one would open the door. But they did not. She continued to read.

Still, I will hold faith to the spirit in which we left things between us and continue to hope that upon acquainting yourself more with my character, we might both come to the same conclusion. I ought now to give you thanks because your even-mindedness inspired me to conduct a deeper introspection. While I found no defects of my affections, I also reasoned that my existing sentiments toward you can feel no threat from the passage of time and distance. If however, the sentiments that I shared yesterday are not of a steady manner after these weeks of separation, then I should hardly be able to say that I ever deserved your regard. In professing honesty, requesting accommodation for your own reasons, you have provided me a test of my mettle. Please do not misunderstand me; I do not believe you requested a delay in our conversation in a deceitful ploy in the arts of matchmaking. You honored me by sharing your burden and I wish only to make it lighter.

Feeling her emotions run from anger to delight, Elizabeth blinked furiously frustrated with the pangs of regret. Her feelings for Mr. Darcy, entirely unfounded judged by length of acquaintance, made her question her simpleness in requesting the delay in the first place! She had not confessed to him fleeting fancies of her youth and how she was now excessively analyzing her own behavior and his for some signs of regard. In that inspection, she had to admit, never had she felt this hollow ache she suffered now: a yearning for assurances of when she would be in Mr. Darcy's presence once more. Her reaction once more granted trust in her heart's interest from a point of reasonable deduction.

I find myself armed with pen and parchment more at ease to express my thoughts and conflictions about the subjects you raised in our time together in the churchyard. I do not wish for you to suppose one concern is higher magnitude than the other due to the order in which I discuss them, only that your words yesterday afternoon have stirred new standards for my consideration in which I judge my behavior. I humbly beg for your indulgence of my exploration of these matters and grant it your justice that I am to share as freely and honestly as you afforded me.

You laid a charge at my feet about choosing to travel without my sister. At first, I admit I was angry for you to even raise the subject, but that was unfair as there was no way for you to know of the great strain and near loss I experienced this past summer in regards to her. When my father died five years ago, I, along with my cousin Colonel Fitzwilliam, was appointed guardian of my minor sister. For over half a decade, he and I have taken great pains to provide Georgiana with the best tutors and schooling and at times, insulation from our most forceful relatives. I am in possession of a particularly opinionated aunt who will not listen when others disagree with her assumptions and has gone so far as to claim I am engaged to her daughter when I could not be furthest from such a status. On my annual visits to her estate in Kent, a home called Rosings, I began excluding my younger sister because of the effects on Georgiana's disposition. Lady Catherine de Bourgh was particularly close to her sister, my mother, and she made the egregious error in telling my sister that her birth was the chief reason my mother never recovered and died at a young age. Even if there was a shred of truth in her belief, such a declaration to a young lady of a tender age was wholly unacceptable in my opinion. Unfortunately, I continue to visit despite my aunt's increasing delusions to the world around her. I believed her harmless. She never came to London and I never expected any of her sycophants to ever venture outside of her limited domain. For visits in the last few years, I have always taken along my cousin, Colonel Fitzwilliam, or his elder brother, so as to have a second report if one was ever needed.

Elizabeth caught herself nodding, as she wholly believed Mr. Darcy's account of his aunt after listening to her cousin rave about the lady. Her cousin's judgment she valued not a whit, so it only stood to reason that the exact opposite of his claims be true about the woman.

Perhaps one of my greatest weaknesses is in providing service to others without full consideration of the consequences. I believe you and I can think of a particular situation in recent memory where I allowed my desire to save another from pain and suffering to trump any rational discourse. We both can agree charging back into that tavern achieved results few on the surface would ever disparage. But my officiousness after in regards to Dr. Stevens was perhaps an example where I allowed expediency to overrule efficacy. In a similar manner, my cousin and I made plans for my sister to holiday in Ramsgate over the summer. We hired a companion, a Mrs. Younge, who I now believe may not have been the widow she professed to be.

This weakness I hold, I can trace directly to the nature of my father, a man of great fortune who never withheld his assistance to any in need under his purview. Our property in Derbyshire, was run for numerous decades by a very capable man, Mr. John Wickham. He married and had a son in the same year that my parents were blessed with my presence after a number of disappointments. My father happily agreed to be of service as the younger Wickham's godfather, liberally bestowing upon him all of the kindness within his power to grant. Apart from paying for his schooling, my father also appreciated George Wickham's company and manners, finding the man more engaging than myself. I possess no disillusion that where my acts of service derive from my father, my reserved nature I inherited directly from my mother.

Elizabeth snorted at the cavalier nature in which Mr. Darcy described his faults, so flawlessly as something no one might find real fault at all! She smirked and gazed up, out the window to the sight of farm hands and other servants seeing to their morning chores. Memory of their conversation in the church yard brought understanding. She had challenged him on a fault of hers, so perhaps he felt he needed to humble himself in return. And in the line of thinking, Elizabeth realized her fault was also not one she believed was a hindrance with all sincerity. Certainly a problem for others, but never for herself.

When my father died, it was his greatest wish for Mr. George Wickham to take the church as his profession. I, who had observed Mr. Wickham in the unguarded moments afforded another young man close to his age, knew for many years such a profession was unfitting. Therefore it was a great relief that Mr. Wickham asked for a sum in an amount equivalent to the living my father had hoped he might take, intending to study the law. I rather wished, than believed him to be sincere; but at any rate, was perfectly ready to accede to his proposal. I believe we both can agree that some men should not become clergymen.

I believed all connection between us now dissolved. I thought too ill of him to invite him to Pemberley, or admit his society in town. Sadly, his life in town studying the law was merely a pretense. I shall not share the depths of degradation the man sunk to, but suffice to say there was little to no means of redeeming him. Then, the man who held the living my father intended for Mr. Wickham passed away three years ago. He claimed his circumstances were exceedingly bad, and I had a difficulty believing him. He had found the law a most unprofitable study, and was now absolutely resolved on being ordained, if I would present him the living in question. He even went so far as to invoke my revered father's intentions in hopes of persuading me to his argument. You will hardly blame me for refusing to comply with his entreaty, or for resisting the numerous repetitions he made. I imagine his resentment was in proportion to the distress of his circumstances—and he was doubtless as violent in his abuse of me to others.

After this period, I dropped every appearance of acquaintance with the man. That was until this past summer. This year was to be the first one of my sister's establishment to afford her the best education of not only the masters, but also in the skills of comportment and social graces that a school cannot provide. I had agreed to help my friend, Charles Bingley, inspect and find an estate for his permanent residence. We spent most of the summer traveling a number of dilapidated and otherwise distressed Country homes and holdings of illustrious families facing undesired circumstances. Whilst I was performing in the service of a friend, the man I penned so many lines about above ingratiated himself with Mrs. Younge and my sister. My sister possesses an affectionate heart and retained a strong impression of his kindness to her as a child, so it was not difficult for him to persuade her to believe she was in love. They formed a plan to elope. She was then but fifteen, but I give her credit that it was by her I learned of the plan.

Gasping at such a tale, Elizabeth panicked when she heard the mumbles of Jane behind her. She froze and counted to ten, hoping her sister would sleep just a little longer to grant her the time she needed. When Jane did not stir further, Elizabeth began to read at a quicker pace.

Unexpectedly, I surprised her with a visit a day or two before the intended elopement. My sister's guilt over the idea of grieving and offending a brother whom she almost looked up to as a father, brought her to confess all to me. Mr. Wickham abandoned the area, and Mrs. Younge was of course removed from her charge. The intention to preserve my sister's reputation prevented me from any public exposure of the man's misdeeds. Apart from my cousin and the bad actors in the plot, you are the first to know of this painful experience I shoulder. Shortly thereafter, Mr. Bingley wrote to me about one last estate, Netherfield Park.

In order to keep up appearances that nothing was amiss, I hastily traveled with my sister from Ramsgate to the meeting with the land agent and your uncle. Thankfully, I was able to secure the services of another woman, Mrs. Annesley, a woman who's departed husband served with my cousin in the Peninsular War. I then escorted them both up to Pemberley where I could be assured of my sister's safety. Rejoining Mr. Bingley's party at Netherfield Park, with Georgiana safely in Pemberley, even if gossip was begun by Mr. Wickham or Mrs. Younge, it could hardly be believed. My cousin and I could easily say we had planned on placing Georgiana at Ramsgate for the summer, but instead had her spend the summer at home.

Wiping away her tears, Elizabeth easily envisioned her youngest sister, Lydia, listening to the romantic nonsense of a man thinking it great fun to run off and wed without proper approval. Or perhaps even Kitty, the two of them often engaged in such flirtatious behavior. Elizabeth felt gratitude the rumor of a regiment of officers wintering in Meryton proved false. A bawdy group of men without scruples was the last thing her sisters needed as a distraction.

Another matter entirely is one I bring up hesitantly, as I believe perhaps another misunderstanding passed between us. While I would never ascribe blame in a letter where I am not afforded the pleasure of your immediate response, would you perhaps suspend a small amount of consideration in my direction. It was my mistake to even attempt to press my suit when I had learned you were just subjected to your cousin's undoubtedly offensive exercise in the same. However, the offense he gave may have influenced the reception of my statement about why I did not ask for your hand the night I dined at Longbourn. Yes, I can enumerate the large span from my fortune to your family's circumstances. Others in my situation might feel pride or superiority in rejecting for consideration ladies of lesser dowries. In faith, I might be one of those men if I met you some years earlier.

Elizabeth's breathing became labored as she tried to follow his request to suspend a small amount of consideration for him. Her hands gripped the letter more tightly than perhaps prudent and her knuckles began to feel the strain.

Thankfully, I have spent all the time I care to spend as an eligible bachelor in the ballrooms of London. I purposely keep company with Mr. Bingley to avoid such obligations as dances and dinners with many who seek my favor, but not my friendship. I was rude to you on our first meeting and you gave me the cut directly back. I wish that I could claim such behavior was new for me, or that others had given me a similar taste of consequence. Instead, it was quite opposite. For years, I could behave abominably as those situations made me feel, and still receive invitation after invitation.

Furthermore, my mother's family, despite boasting a hereditary title that will never pass to me, Lord willing, pales in holdings compared to my father's lands. The coffers of Pemberley restored a great glory to my grandfather's position, a legacy my uncle, the Earl, now enjoys. I would stand as an unpardonable hypocrite to claim a loftier stock than that of a gentleman's son. In so much as I am aware, you are a gentleman's daughter. Perhaps I hold a greater claim to being the grandson of an earl, but I have yet to see that distinction grant my cousin, Colonel Fitzwilliam, favors or deference as the son of an earl, albeit second in birth order, over my position as the wealthy son of a gentleman.

Forgive me for again assuming a position of confidence you have neither afforded me nor promised. But if you should allow me the chance to make a case for my suit, please know that settlement papers would never place you in a similar position as your mother. As my wife, you would never want for any comfort, and I would provide a trust of funds for use only at your discretion.

"Lizzy? Has Aunt Gardiner written to you?" Jane said, startling her sister to jump in her chair.

Guilty of reading a letter she should have rightfully handed to her father for inspection before her own, Elizabeth blanched.

"Lizzy?"

"Please Jane, Father gave permission for Mr. Darcy to write to me. But I don't want anyone else to know."

Jane squealed in delight but her sister emphatically shook her head.

"It is as I said yesterday, Mr. Darcy and I are friends."

Smiling, Jane rapidly patted her hands together as though she orchestrated some scheme.

"But he writes to you, surely you are engaged," she reasoned.

"No. We are not. And we might never become so," Elizabeth cautioned, feeling her stomach growl in protest.

Jane looked at her sister skeptically, but left her to begin her morning toilette.

Quickly, Elizabeth read the rest of the letter.

I leave you now without enough regulation to stay my hand in expressing once more that I hold you in such high admiration. My heart aches in our separa-

tion though I insist on convincing it otherwise that this is just another exercise in strengthening my resolve. I plan to return to Netherfield Park in a few weeks, after Christmas. I pray that you remain healthy and well, and will still receive my calls when such a time comes. I dare not feel so bold as to receive a letter back, but if you'd like, I have left my direction. I will only add, God bless you.

Fitzwilliam Darcy.

Hastily folding the letter, she summarized the contents for Jane: "He writes that he will return after Christmas, and he is most anxious to see his sister at Pemberley."

Jane splashed water on her face over the bowl on their vanity. After she patted her skin dry, she turned to address her sister.

"I'm sure Charles will be surprised I know such intelligence before he tells me," she said, softly.

"Jane, you mustn't! Please, you cannot say a word about the letter to anyone else."

"But why? Mr. Darcy is a good man, Lizzy. You cannot wish to live here at Longbourn forever," Jane said, then paused. "Or else you would have accepted Mr. Collins."

"Could you have accepted Mr. Collins?" Elizabeth asked, still holding Mr. Darcy's letter in her hand.

Jane remained silent but her mouth twisted into a brief flash of disgust before she plastered an expression of polite comportment across her face. "I only want you to be happy, as happy as I am."

Elizabeth grumbled as she fumbled with the lock on her trunk resting on her side of the room. "You forget I was unconscious or indisposed half of the time we have even known the gentlemen," she argued. Finally, the tight mechanism gave and she could lift the lid on her gift from her last birthday. Both girls kept correspondence and treasures they did not want borrowed by their younger sisters in their respective trunks. The small act of privacy never offended each other.

Before tucking the letter away, Elizabeth paused as she stared at the stacks of letters from Charlotte, letters she would never add another piece of parchment to the carefully bound grouping.

"Lizzy?" Jane asked, as her sister began to sniffle.

Wiping her nose unceremoniously with the

sleeve of her gown, Elizabeth sniffed to restore her countenance.

"I am well," she fibbed. Then placed the letter underneath Charlotte's missives and closed the lid. "Did I tell you I have resolved to paint for Sir William and Lady Lucas?"

CHAPTER 17

Mr. Collins abandoned his efforts to unite himself with the Bennet family through marriage without any further offers to his cousins. Farewelling the family as he planned just a fortnight away from his patroness, no one but Mary seemed to miss his presence. The family enjoyed a short lull in social obligations until excitement for Jane's wedding and Elizabeth's recovery spilled over into the seasonal traditions of Longbourn.

Evergreens adorned the house from top to bottom. Elizabeth could not walk into a room without the pungent freshness of the forest assaulting her senses, reminding her of why she loved the holiday best. As the weather grew worse for her daily walks, the reminder of the woods and glens she frequented coming indoors offered a partial consolation. In a week, it would be Christmas, and then Jane and Mr. Bingley would marry. Though she felt most anxious for her sister's happiness, it was the return of Mr. Darcy's presence to the neighborhood, as he promised, that ignited her own.

During their separation, Mr. Bennet shared a few lines that directly related to Elizabeth from the letters he received from Mr. Darcy with her. While Elizabeth wished to hear more than short hopes for her continued good health, she realized that Mr. Darcy was unlikely to write any lines of substance that her father might read. Each time she was summoned to the library that Mr. Bennet used as his study, her father greatly enjoyed embarrassing his daughter to the fullest extent.

"So Lizzy, your sister is crossed in love. Next to being married, a state she will soon enter in good time, a girl likes to be crossed in love now and then."

"Father," Elizabeth attempted to interrupt him, but he would not be dissuaded from his point.

"It is something to think of, and it gives her a sort of distinction among her companions. When is your turn to come? You will hardly bear to be outdone by Jane for long."

Elizabeth frowned at her father. She gazed down at her hands stained in the hues of burnt umber, all the way underneath her fingernails. She sighed as she wished she had not been summoned at all, as her project above stairs had served most faithfully in excusing her from Jane's wedding activities. She needed to complete it if she hoped to present it to the Lucas family before Christmas.

"I am not in competition with my sister," she said, plainly. Then she looked up to her father. "And if I was, Jane would surely lose. You know she cannot bear to disappoint anyone, not even in her own self-interest."

Mr. Bennet waved off his daughter's logic. "Now is your time. Let Darcy be your man. Surely you have some yearnings in that heart of yours to commit to paper that I may send back to him?" Mr. Bennet scowled as Elizabeth laughed at him, shaking her head.

"The yearnings of my heart, sir, do not belong in a letter to a man I am not presently engaged with."

"Then write to the man about the weather! Your painting! Anything, in faith, my daughter, so that I do not yet have to write to him again!"

Elizabeth smiled. Certainly, her father would

not outright offer falsehoods if he did not wish to encourage her with Mr. Darcy. But the true dilemma he faced was not in fostering that man's feelings, but to avoid writing more correspondence. And thus far, Mr. Darcy had been a very reliable correspondent with at least one letter reaching Longbourn each week.

"I will pen him my thanks for his gift and detail the work I am pursuing, after," she stressed the last word, "I have finished and presented the painting to the Lucases."

"But how long will that put off a response to Mr. Darcy?" Mr. Bennet asked, suspiciously.

"I believe I can finish today and allow it to cure enough to travel in two days."

Mr. Bennet groaned, covering his face with his hands. "By then he will have surely sent another letter!"

Elizabeth hesitated, not wishing to give her father any further material to tease her upon. Still, she ached to know the answer to her question.

"Does Mr. Darcy write about his plans to travel back to Hertfordshire?" She tried to sound as unaffected as she could manage, and looked away from her father to reveal none of her emotions on her face.

Mr. Bennet did not answer and allowed silence to hang in the room. His daughter's question caught him quite off guard. Clearing his throat, as the implications soon troubled his mind, he gave his daughter honesty.

"He has mentioned it occurring, but as to any specific dates, I'm afraid not."

Elizabeth closed her eyes as her father tried to reassure her that such an oversight meant nothing at all. The man did not intend to stay at Longbourn, and being the great man that Mr. Darcy was, he certainly would not believe he needed to submit his travel plans to a leaky baronet in the middle of nowhere of note, England.

Mumbling something in agreement, she politely abandoned her father to see about her own business: the gift she planned for Sir William Lucas and Lady Lucas. Once started, her paintings called out to her throughout the day in her mind as small fixes and embellishments took form in her imagination.

Upstairs, Jane occupied their room allowing their shared maid to style her hair.

"Is Mama parading you about again?" Elizabeth asked, lifting her apron over her head that she wore when she painted. She scowled to find that in the time she had visited with her father, at his behest, the sun's position in the sky changed the lighting in the studio area of their room. Wrestling with her easel, Elizabeth listened as Jane answered.

"We are visiting Mrs. Long. Mama is insistent that I visit the many families in the area to establish myself as the future Mrs. Bingley."

"While you each wear gray, how could anyone suspect such a joyous occasion is nearly upon us?" Elizabeth nudged the legs of her easel with her foot to get the best light on the portion of Maria Lucas' gown that she was working on. At first, she had thought to paint them in the gowns from the assembly, but that would always make the painting a source of melancholy. Instead, Elizabeth depicted each Lucas daughter wearing the frock she remembered flattering them best. However, the pale pink of Maria's gown had proved to be the most aggravating shade to capture.

"I'm also not so sure Mr. Bingley will remain in the area," Jane braved explaining after the maid left them.

Elizabeth paused in her mixing of pigments. "Strange. I believed with Mr. Bingley offering for your hand, his decision to purchase Netherfield Park a foregone conclusion."

Jane shook her head. "We've spoken, and he asked me if I should like to remain in Hertfordshire."

"And what did you tell him?"

Jane shrugged, gathering the last of the things she needed before a visit. "If you marry Mr. Darcy, you will be far away to the north."

Elizabeth pursed her lips as her sister's obvious logic challenged her desires. She loved the idea of marrying Mr. Darcy and playing mistress to a mystery estate far away. The practicality of such a vocation, however, warred with her familiarity of her surroundings, in addition to the love she felt for her family.

"I hadn't given that much consideration," was the only noncommittal response she offered.

Jane approached Elizabeth's painting to see the progress, one of the only family members permitted to witness a work before completion. Truthfully, the permission derived from the realities of sharing a bedroom instead of the artist's own preference.

"Charlotte's expression is sublime," Jane complimented, earning a nod from her sister. Suddenly, Jane spotted a small detail that was out of place. "I don't recall her wearing a cross similar to yours."

"I painted mine on her."

Jane gulped as Elizabeth's stony expression remained fixed on painting the ruffles of Maria's hemline.

"That is a lovely touch."

Hearing their mother bellow up the stairs, Jane reluctantly left her younger sister to her enterprise. Picking up another paintbrush, and placing the handle of the previous one between her teeth for easy retrieval, Elizabeth delicately moved the paint into a simulation of movement. Still, her mind raced over Jane's intelligence that she and Mr. Bingley might move away. This notion compounded with the added reminder that to marry Mr. Darcy, she, too, would by necessity have to move away from Longbourn. She equally felt silly to find herself stuck upon these two ideas, as there was nothing plainer about the business of marriage than a bride leaving her family to join her groom.

Setting her brushes down and stretching her neck to relieve herself of the tightness growing between her shoulder blades, she inspected the small inventory of blank canvases in her possession. Instead of giving over to dismay about the inability to live in two places at once, she assigned herself a new mission to complete after the Lucas painting.

She would paint her favorite places near her home so that no matter where she lived in all of England, a part of her home would travel with her. The new project, already demanding space in the artist's mind, made Elizabeth sigh with resignation. She would have to paint from near dawn until dusk to finish all of them if Mr. Darcy wanted a short engagement like Mr. Bingley!

CHAPTER 18

The mood at Lucas Lodge contrasted greatly with the emotional atmosphere Elizabeth Bennet experienced at Longbourn. For the first time since the fire, Elizabeth felt as though she was not alone in her bereavement over the loss of life that night. Granted, it was slightly unfair to chastise her family's lack of mourning period when the Lucas family had lost so much while the Bennet family suffered but one loss and not that of a daughter.

Even securing the audience to present her painting had proven to be difficult. Lady Lucas' first response expressed that she was not accepting visitors of any kind. It was only after Elizabeth wrote back that she desperately needed to see the family as she possessed something of

Charlotte's she thought the family might like returned that she was granted a time to visit the week before Christmas. She didn't say it was her likeness and not a trinket or other treasured possession.

To her surprise, Sir William Lucas wasted no time after receiving the painting to find it a place of honor. He hastily yanked down an ill-famed depiction of a relative Charlotte had never mentioned over the mantle. In its place, Elizabeth's work was hung with great reverence. For some reason, this embarrassed her greatly. In her mind, she thought the Lucases would have placed the painting in their bedroom, or some other private room away from the eyes of casual visitors.

"However did you capture them so expertly?" Lady Lucas asked, still dabbing her eyes from tears of happiness.

Elizabeth chuckled nervously. "Charlotte and Maria often posed for me. All of those picnics and hikes up Oakham Mount. I miss them so much, you see." Her voice choked in her throat. She swallowed and continued on. "But I never dispose of a sketchbook. Even the sketches I loathe to claim as done by my hand. Later I always discover at least a handful of pages in each holds works I am proud of," she babbled, realizing that she was losing Lady Lucas in her explanation.

Quickly, she simplified her answer. "I used several sketches, and my own memories, for the painting."

"I don't believe we would have a more faithful rendering than if our girls had sat for a master portraitist," Sir William Lucas offered high praise, holding his wife in an embrace.

Not wishing to overstay her welcome, Elizabeth craned her neck to spy John Lucas passing by the parlor, refusing to be a part of the awkward memorial inside.

"Thank you for accepting my small offering," she began, only to be interrupted by both of Charlotte's parents that she accept the gratitude from them and not the other way around. Elizabeth took one last look at the calming expression of her closest friends, and then still offered her condolences to the Lucas family for their loss.

As Charlotte's parents wept anew over the painting of their daughters lost in the fire, Elizabeth quietly stepped away to catch John in the hall.

"Would you be so kind as to call my carriage?" she asked her dearest friend's eldest brother.

John Lucas offered a small bow of his head in agreement. When he did not speak, Elizabeth grew irritated and addressed him again.

"I should have inquired before this time as to your health," she said, modestly.

"And how should you have inquired? While you were fighting to survive yourself, or later when you took ill with fever?" John Lucas asked, revealing that he had remained aware, somehow, of her situation at Longbourn.

John Lucas walked past Elizabeth to the footman he saw crossing to the back of Lucas Lodge. With a whisper, he made the lady's request for her family's vehicle to be brought around to the front. Standing with his back to Elizabeth, he hunched his shoulders and his body shook with silent sobs.

"John?" she asked, slowly walking towards him where they could see his parents and the painting through a clear line of sight.

He flinched as she touched his shoulder with her gloved hand. With a loud sniff, John Lucas regained his composure and wiped his face with a handkerchief.

"Your painting is superb. We do not deserve such kindness," he said.

"I was too late to save them," she said.

"No, the failing is mine," he said tersely, finally turning to face her.

Startled by the pain twisted in his face, Elizabeth gasped.

"We were all lucky to survive that night. But just the same," she said, lowering her voice to a whisper, "I feel the guilt as you do."

"Do you? Could you possibly? How many sisters did you lose? How many sisters did you abandon for a silly dance around a circle because you wanted to tease a friend?" he spat the rhetorical questions, forcing Elizabeth to blink back tears.

"Yes, we all danced as we were expected. But that doesn't mean that you abandoned your sisters."

"I ran like a coward," he confessed. "I was no hero like the other gentlemen."

Elizabeth's head began to pound from the tension tightening at the base of her neck. "You could not have saved them. I went back in," she began, but John Lucas threw up his hands and began to walk away from her. Elizabeth chased after him. "No, listen!" she demanded, grabbing his arm. "They had both succumbed by the time I found them. I couldn't stand to look at myself in the mirror until I finished this painting. But the truth is, the truth is," she said, gasping for breath.

Sir William Lucas and Lady Lucas had grown curious by the commotion in the hall and now witnessed the exchange from the doorway.

"The truth is I killed my sisters!" John Lucas shouted.

But Elizabeth met him in volume.

"You fool! Had you gone back in, I would have had to paint you as well! Your family would have lost even more!"

John Lucas froze as his parents stared at him.

"Is that what you believe, my son? That you failed them? Us?" Lady Lucas asked gently as her son's posture again slumped under the heavy weight of survivor's guilt.

Elizabeth caught his eye and silently pleaded with him to listen.

"I never re-entered the building. I couldn't find them in the escape, and then when I realized they were not outside, I didn't go back in," he explained.

Sir William Lucas began to berate his son for such foolish thinking as well, enumerating the deaths that came from precisely such foolhardy behavior.

"And I should have been one of them, if not

for Mr. Darcy," Elizabeth shared, supporting John's parents in their logic.

Slowly, John Lucas began to hear their words and admitted that he had carried around an unearned burden of responsibility. Sir William Lucas clasped his son's shoulders and led him into the parlor, forcing him to finally look at the portrait of Charlotte and Maria properly.

"There, my boy, see? See their smiles? Where they are now, I have no doubt, is a place of happiness and joy. Look at your sisters and know they feel no pain," he reasoned.

Suddenly feeling as though she was absolutely imposing on the family's grief, Elizabeth felt relieved when a footman appeared to announce her carriage was ready. Before she could leave, Lady Lucas grasped her hands.

"I forgot to say how sorry I am for your family's loss. Mrs. Phillips' light and cheerful disposition will be sorely missed in this community."

Elizabeth nodded. "My uncle is beside himself with grief. And my mother has struggled to honor her sister while supporting Jane's engagement."

Lady Lucas nodded in understanding. "Thank you, not just for the painting, but for confronting

John. We had no idea how he felt about that night. He refused to speak of it."

Weakly, Elizabeth smiled. "None of us want to believe there wasn't more we could do. But if my sister Jane can find happiness so soon after such a tragedy, maybe there is hope for the rest of us."

"Indeed," Lady Lucas agreed. "I should call upon your mother. Perhaps she and I could provide each other comfort."

"Yes, I believe she would dearly love that. Jane is to marry next week, and I fear she will take it as yet another loss."

Lady Lucas grimaced and Elizabeth felt embarrassed for reminding her of such a happy event her daughters never experienced. Still, the lady recovered her manners. "Mr. Bingley seems to be a very nice man. He called after the fire to see if our family needed anything after the, after the . . ." she said, struggling to finish her thought.

Shocking poor Lady Lucas out of her melancholy, Elizabeth laughed. "Yes, I would say that is high praise coming from him as I can hardly imagine a moment he hasn't been at Longbourn making a nuisance of himself!"

Stunned at first by Elizabeth's rhetoric, Lady Lucas soon joined her daughter's friend in laughter.

"Your poor father!" she exclaimed and Elizabeth bobbed her head enthusiastically in agreement.

"He has suffered most acutely for my sister's future happiness," she stated.

Finally, Lady Lucas followed Elizabeth as she walked towards the door to leave Lucas Lodge.

"I hope you will also come to visit more. I know Charlotte is not here," Lady Lucas managed, taking a pause as it was new to speak about her daughter in the past tense to others. "I have such fond memories of the two of you growing up. I sincerely hope that you will continue to visit from time to time and allow me to be reminded of those happier days."

Elizabeth started to promise she would make such an effort, but the words caught in her throat. How could she promise to Lady Lucas she would visit when her hope was to move away with Mr. Darcy? Not wishing for her personal business to become fodder for gossip, she took a moment to look down and make sure she had her shawl and reticule firmly in her hand as though checking before taking her leave.

"Yes, I shall make an effort to visit more and will send a note ahead in case you are not quite up to experiencing those happier moments that day," she offered, judiciously.

Enjoying the quiet ride back to Longbourn in a rare moment alone in her family's carriage, Elizabeth allowed the gentle rocking to lull herself into a stupor. She closed her eyes and for once, the horrors of that night did not flash before them. Her heart finally felt unburdened, though she would never have believed her friend Charlotte capable of haunting someone, she laughed to herself as that was precisely how she felt at that moment. Her friend's spirit asked nothing more, Elizabeth was free.

CHAPTER 19

Emotionally exhausted, stepping one foot over the threshold of her father's home, Elizabeth could sense something was terribly wrong.

"There you are!"

Elizabeth winced as her mother thundered down the stairs with great haste before she could escape down the hall to her father's library. Still, the speed of her mother's movements didn't prevent her from gazing forlornly in the direction of her usual sanctuary. Her mother caught on immediately to her daughter's aims.

"Oho, do not go looking for your father, he cannot save you," Mrs. Bennet stated, grasping her daughter's elbow to pull her away from the hallway. "Truly, Lizzy, I will never understand you. I did everything I could on your behalf for your cousin, Mr. Collins, to take you on."

"But Mama," Elizabeth said, wrestling her elbow free with little effort. "I did not love him."

Mrs. Bennet stopped and turned to her daughter, staring at her with a look of utter incredulity. "You would have had this house! You would have stayed with your father and me! Of course, you did not love him! Who said anything about loving him? But in marrying him you would have had a comfortable home and a husband of good character."

"But I would not have been happy," Elizabeth tried to argue, unsure why her mother was suddenly arguing with her again about Mr. Collins more than a month after his failed proposal.

Mrs. Bennet continued to usher her daughter towards the closed parlor doors. "None of us are assured happiness, child. It's a matter of chance in a marriage," she said, off-handed before taking a deep breath and then opening the parlor door. "My daughter has returned your Ladyship," she began, entering the room and offering a curtsy.

Pure curiosity attracted Elizabeth to stand next to her mother and curtsy to the finely dressed woman sitting on the sofa that she had not been given an introduction to.

"You are Elizabeth Bennet?" the woman asked, sharp in her tone.

Dumbly, Elizabeth nodded, her eyes falling to the woman's bejeweled hand laboring to hold the ornate orb of a walking stick. Her eyes widened as she watched the woman twist and turn the stick in agitation, recalling how she imagined herself using such a tool. Thankfully, she hadn't needed the aid of a stick in over a week to keep her balance upon her feet.

"You may leave us, I should like to speak to your daughter alone," the stranger demanded.

Mrs. Bennet began to take her leave, but Elizabeth put aside her manners for her own protection. She had no earthly idea who this woman was, and the last thing she wanted was to be left alone with her. Frantically, her mind raced for an explanation, and processing her mother's chastisement in the foyer, she suddenly worried that she was being handed over as a lady's companion to this perfect stranger!

"Mama, please, I should like for you to stay. Mrs... " Elizabeth trailed off as she emphasized her lack of knowledge as to the visitor's name.

"Lady Catherine de Bourgh!" the woman practically shouted, banging her walking stick into the rug.

The name sent a jolt of fear down Elizabeth's spine and she whipped her head to face the threatening woman. Lines from Mr. Darcy's letter describing the woman as suffering delusions brought on a touch of fear. She no longer worried about being made a lady's companion, but that the woman might try to force her parents to make her marry Mr. Collins!

"Please, sit with me and Lady Catherine de Bourgh for our visit," Elizabeth said, not taking her eyes off the grand lady, and stepping sideways to loop her arm into her mother's. Directing Mrs. Bennet to the sofa to sit next to her ladyship, a stroke to her ego she could not resist, Elizabeth retreated to the chair in the corner, nearest the door. Without asking permission, she took a seat.

"I would prefer to speak to you alone, Miss Bennet," Lady Catherine again stated. Willfully misunderstanding the woman, Elizabeth offered to fetch her sister Jane, only irritating the woman further. Finding she now understood more her father's habits of poking and taunting others in social situations, as her father's daughter, Elizabeth remained stubborn in her desires.

"Forgive me, your Ladyship, but as we are not

yet well-acquainted, you must agree that a young woman such as myself would rely upon my mother in circumstances such as these," she reasoned.

Mrs. Bennet cooed over her daughter, joining in the convincing of Lady Catherine to satisfy all of their curiosities as to why she visited Longbourn in the first place. "How is our cousin, Mr. Collins? Well, I hope since he has returned to you?" she asked.

"Relating the health of Mr. Collins is not why I have come," she retorted to Mrs. Bennet, then returned her focus to Elizabeth. "You can be at no loss, Miss Bennet, to understand the reason of my journey hither. Your own heart, your own conscience, must tell you why I come."

"Indeed, you are mistaken, Madam. I have not been at all able to account for the honor of seeing you here," Elizabeth replied, keeping her tone respectful, though she began to suspect that the very cousin they inquired about had told tales to his patroness regarding herself and Mr. Darcy.

"Miss Bennet," replied her ladyship, in an angry tone, "you ought to know, I am not to be trifled with. But however insincere you may choose to be, you shall not find me so. My character has ever been celebrated for its sincerity and frankness, and in a cause of such moment as this, I shall certainly not depart from it. A report of a most alarming nature reached me two days ago. I was told that not only your sister was on the point of being most advantageously married, but that you, Miss Elizabeth Bennet, would, in all likelihood, be soon afterwards united to my nephew, my own nephew, Mr. Darcy. Though I know it must be a scandalous falsehood, though I would not injure him so much as to suppose the truth of it possible, I instantly resolved on setting off for this place, that I might make my sentiments known to you."

Mrs. Bennet gasped. "Lizzy! Why did you not tell me you are engaged to Mr. Darcy?" she squealed.

Elizabeth made the smallest shake of her head to still her mother's jubilation but to no avail. She decided to try distraction. "Yes, my sister is on the point of being most advantageously married to Mr. Bingley, isn't she Mama?"

The question was all of the encouragement her mother needed. She began to expound about Mr. Darcy's friend, Mr. Bingley, and how her sweet Jane and the gentleman in question were to wed the following week.

"After the Christmas holidays, of course, as

my brother in Town is to visit with his family. My husband has not placed the announcement in the London papers, you see, but the second of January is to be Jane's day."

"Madam, I am not here to discuss your daughter Jane. There," Lady Catherine turned her attention back to her perceived adversary. "Your mother has outed your scheme and confirmed you are engaged to my nephew! This is not to be borne. Are the shades of Pemberley to be thus polluted?"

Elizabeth was about to argue with the grand woman that her mother was mistaken, she was not presently engaged to Mr. Darcy. But she was not so quick as Franny Bennet in protecting her young.

"I must have misunderstood you, your Ladyship. Surely you have come here to congratulate my daughter on her engagement to your nephew."

"Let me be rightly understood. This match, to which you have the presumption to aspire, can never take place. No, never. Mr. Darcy is engaged to my daughter."

Mrs. Bennet scoffed in shock. She met the grand lady eye-to-eye, challenging her to back up her claim. "If he is so, Mr. Darcy could never have made an offer to my daughter. The man I met was the very depiction of honor and integrity. Did you know he saved Lizzy from a fire?"

Lady Catherine de Bourgh held her breath in anger, allowing her cheeks to appear scorched in color before blowing out a breath. "The engagement between them is of a peculiar kind. From their infancy, they have been intended for each other. It was the favorite wish of his mother, as well as mine. While in their cradles, we planned the union: and now, at the moment when the wishes of both sisters would be accomplished in their marriage, to be prevented by a young woman of inferior birth, of no importance in the world, and wholly unallied to the family!" Lady Catherine blustered on, and spying no reaction from Elizabeth that resembled fear, she attempted to scare her mother. "As a mother, do you wish for your daughter to be ostracized and rejected in her marriage? Do you pay no regard to the wishes of his friends? To his tacit engagement with Miss De Bourgh? Are you lost to every feeling of propriety and delicacy? Have you not heard me say that from his earliest hours he was destined for his cousin?"

Mrs. Bennet nodded her head, appearing to agree with Lady Catherine. But her words said otherwise. "Having just lost my sister, I can sympathize in the pain of being unable to fulfill her dying wish. My sister died childless, you see. However, if Mr. Darcy is neither by honor nor inclination confined to his cousin, why is he not to make another choice? And if my daughter is that choice, why may she not accept him?"

The words of her mother cut Elizabeth's heart to ribbons. She listened with mortification as the two older women argued over the most ironic of circumstances. She was not engaged to Mr. Darcy. While she had not rejected him, as she had not received a full offer of his hand, she knew her mother's question to be so close to the truth that it might as well have been so. She had not accepted him, foolishly, obstinately, and in such a head-strong manner, he might have second thoughts about ever returning to Meryton if he thought carefully about it.

"Stop, please, just stop!" Elizabeth pleaded, as the two women finally looked at her. They had just traded further barbs about Elizabeth being censured and slighted by all and Mrs. Bennet insisting that as a gentleman's daughter, Elizabeth was of the same social sphere as Mr. Darcy.

Swallowing down her utter distaste for the

entire display, Elizabeth put the entire debate to rest.

"I am not engaged to Mr. Darcy."

Mrs. Bennet gasped, clutching her handkerchief, suddenly glaring meanly at her disloyal daughter who had allowed her to carry on in such a way with a peer. Lady Catherine de Bourgh grinned like a cat who had captured its supper.

"And will you promise me never to enter into such an engagement?"

"I will make no promise of the kind."

Lady Catherine wiggled her enormous body further into the sofa as though she were finding a more comfortable position. One that would allow her to remain in the seat she had claimed. "Miss Bennet I am shocked and astonished. I expected to find a more reasonable young woman. But do not deceive yourself into a belief that I will ever recede. I shall not go away till you have given me the assurance I require."

Stiffly, Elizabeth rose and upon reaching the door, she opened it.

"And I certainly never shall give it. I am not to be intimidated into anything so wholly unreasonable. Your ladyship wants Mr. Darcy to marry your daughter, but would my giving you the wished-for promise make their marriage at all more probable? You have widely mistaken my character, if you think I can be worked on by such persuasions as these. How far your nephew might approve of your interference in *his* affairs, I cannot tell; but you have certainly no right to concern yourself in mine."

She waved her hand, palm up, to signal the door was open for a reason when Lady Catherine did not budge. "I must beg, therefore, to be importuned no farther on the subject."

"Not so hasty, if you please."

Elizabeth ignored the lady's plea and remained standing. Never in her life did she wish for one of her more simple sisters to dash down the stairs and interfere in her business. Keeping her anger in check proved more difficult the longer Lady Catherine spoke.

"I am by no means done. To all the objections I have already urged, I have still another to add. I am no stranger to the particulars of inheritance placed upon this humble estate. Yes, yes, when your father dies, this home shall pass to my lowly parson, a man we can all agree to be no wit. Even should your sister get a son off that Bingley fellow, Mr. Collins has explained the entail is quite specific about lines. Is such a man to be my nephew's family? Imagine the embarrassment he would feel having to dignify the head of his wife's family, a man once in service to his aunt!"

While Elizabeth did not disagree with Lady Catherine that the company of Mr. Collins after her father's death would be undesirable, she believed in her heart that Mr. Darcy could not care about such things.

"You have insulted me in every possible method. I must beg you to leave."

Lady Catherine's frustration finally overset her dwindling patience. The rudeness of being asked to leave by a woman so wholly beneath her inflamed her greatest temper. "You have no regard, then, for the honor and credit of my nephew! Unfeeling, selfish girl! Do you not consider that a connection with you must disgrace him in the eyes of all?"

Elizabeth's mouth twisted into a sly smile to witness her social superior lose her composure. She opted for a small restoration of decorum, just to needle the woman. "Lady Catherine, I have nothing further to say. You know my sentiments."

Mrs. Bennet startled at her daughter's words, feeling a new glimmer of hope. In a small voice, she added her question to the fray. "You are then resolved to have him?"

Both women turned to look at Mrs. Bennet, each surprised by the simple truth vetted out in so much unnecessary and rude discourse.

As Lady Catherine accepted defeat and began to walk slowly to the door, she continued her complaints. "And this is your real opinion! This is your final resolve! Very well. I shall now know how to act. Do not imagine, Miss Bennet, that your ambition will ever be gratified. I came to try you. I hoped to find you reasonable; but, depend upon it, I will carry my point."

Reaching the doorway, where Mr. Bennet stood, as the raised voices had attracted his notice from his sanctuary, he wisely informed her ladyship that her carriage was ready. Quickly they ushered her to the vehicle when suddenly she turned around to have a final word before leaving. "I take no leave of you, Miss Bennet. I send no compliments to your mother. You deserve no such attention. I am most seriously displeased."

"We shall endeavor to labor under the shame of such an outcome as to displease you, your Ladyship," Mr. Bennet said, sarcastically, before bowing to the carriage.

When the vehicle rattled off down the drive, Mr. Bennet finally inquired as to what happened. But his daughter was quite finished with concealments and explanations. She had no doubt that Lady Catherine de Bourgh would hurry on to Pemberley to give her nephew a report of what had occurred, and she worried about the outcome. If Mr. Darcy believed his aunt delusional, how would he ever believe that Elizabeth promised to never promise not to marry him? The more she thought about the lady's threat to carry her point, the more Elizabeth realized the entire mess could grow infinitely worse.

"Father, I must write to Mr. Darcy and send it by messenger."

"Lizzy . . ." he cautioned. "Surely you are not threatened by that saucebox!"

Elizabeth turned away from her father, not offering him further explanation. "I will ask Mama, then. She will agree."

CHAPTER 20

The unannounced arrival of Lady Catherine de Bourgh four days before Christmas startled the staff at Pemberley who believed only their Master, his sister, and her companion, Mrs. Annesley, would be in residence. Mrs. Reynolds, the housekeeper, wasted no time in having rooms made ready for her ladyship and her daughter, Anne, as she welcomed the sister of her former mistress.

"I'm afraid the garden rooms you usually occupy are being refurbished, Your Ladyship," Mrs. Reynolds explained until she was cut off by the most imposing visitor.

"My daughter will stay in the Mistresses suite, and I can take any suite in the family wing," she declared.

Mrs. Reynolds blanched. Upon his arrival some weeks earlier, Mr. Darcy had instructed for the mistress' chambers to be refreshed and some of the new furnishings from other rooms. She worried now that rumors of the Master being betrothed to his cousin were true. The bad memories of waiting on Lady Catherine de Bourgh as a younger maid in the household distracted Nan Reynolds until Lady Catherine again cleared her throat.

"I'm terribly sorry, but the Mistresses suite is also being refurbished. Why don't I show you both to the parlor and have Mr. Darcy told of your arrival."

"Certainly not! I will find my nephew, holed up in that infernal study of his father's, I'm sure. No, Anne, you go to your room and rest. I have a bone of contention with the boy's lack of judgment!" Lady Catherine bellowed, using her walking stick to spryly amble out of the foyer in the direction she planned to investigate.

The young footman, fair in face, new to the ranks of the ground floor service, stood dumbly looking at Mrs. Reynolds for orders, then back at Lady Catherine who reached the door.

"Go," Mrs. Reynolds urged the young man, who hurried to open the door but was too late.

Lady Catherine had huffed her disapproval and yanked open the door herself. She was a woman on a mission, and Mrs. Reynolds was powerless to warn Mr. Darcy.

"My mother is angry. She wants Fitzwilliam to marry me, but he wants to marry another," Anne said, filling Mrs. Reynolds in on the lengthy diatribe she had to hear in the carriage ride the entire way north. "I'll join my cousin, Georgiana, in the music room. I know no one knew we were coming. Until there's a room available," she explained, walking away from the shocked Mrs. Reynolds to take the stairs to the piano scales played above.

Mrs. Reynolds thought to go to Mr. Darcy but calculated she was too late. The sun was already low in the sky, too low for the de Bourgh party to leave that evening if the discussion were to go wrongly. Just as she was about to leave the foyer, another knock sounded on the front door.

"Gracious me, more unscheduled visitors?" she asked, mostly to herself, before motioning for the footman standing by the door to open it.

A man with a low cap and his horse in the drive, behind the carriage still being unloaded, stood without making eye contact.

"A message for Mr. Darcy."

Mrs. Reynolds accepted the simple letter with a direction of Hertfordshire. She reached into her pocket and pulled out some coins for the man. "If you ride around back, tell them Mrs. Reynolds sent you for a meal and bed. You can rest up before leaving in the morning."

"Thank you, Mrs. Reynolds," the rider said, lifting his hat to reveal he was very shabby indeed. But Mrs. Reynolds did not comment on the man's stench or lack of grooming. She turned a keen eye to the footmen unloading the de Bourgh carriage, looking for any signs of laziness. Then missive in hand, she spun on her heel to take the message straight to Mr. Darcy. Lady Catherine de Bourgh would not like it, but her duty was to the Master of Pemberley, not his aunt.

Raised voices inside the study gave Mrs. Reynolds pause when she reached the heavy oak door. The new footman, Henkley, stood listening to every word.

"Go down to the kitchens and tell Cook there will be two more for dinner. And have a tray of refreshments sent to the music room."

The lad looked forlornly at the doors, disliking his new orders when he could so happily remain behind and have plenty of juicy tales to impress the housemaids. But Mrs. Reynolds was insistent. Once alone in the hallway, she listened for a moment to plan her entry for an appropriate lull in the argument.

"And do you know that her mother, her mother tried to insist as a gentleman's daughter, ha!" Lady Catherine shouted, "That as a gentleman's daughter, you two are equals!"

Silence fell for a moment and just as Mrs. Reynolds knocked on the door, she heard Mr. Darcy's reply.

"And what did Miss Elizabeth say to all of this?" he asked. "Enter!"

Mrs. Reynolds opened the door as Lady Catherine ignored the arrival of a servant entirely.

"It does not matter what she said! Anne is here and we are putting an end to your avoiding your duty. You will marry her. Here. I have procured a license," Lady Catherine showed her nephew the document she made her parson, Mr. Collins, draft.

Mr. Darcy frowned as both his aunt and his housekeeper held out documents for his review.

"A message, sir," Mrs. Reynolds offered, as Mr. Darcy made eye contact with her and accepted her letter first. Lady Catherine scoffed at her nephew's impertinence and withdrew the license for his review.

Ignoring his aunt, Darcy opened the slim letter and read the few lines penned within. Absently, his hand slipped into his coat pocket to fondle the well-worn shred of ribbon gifted to him by another. Folding the letter and placing it in his coat pocket, he addressed Mrs. Reynolds.

"My aunt and cousin will stay this evening and ride over to Matlock in the morning. Please advise the stables. And I'd like to see my sister."

Mrs. Reynolds nodded and left the study, but Lady Catherine refused to be set aside.

"Matlock? I have no plans to go there. You shall marry Anne, here. In the same chapel your mother and father were married in."

Mr. Darcy chuckled at his aunt, irritating her further.

"There is only one woman in the world I could ever be prevailed upon to marry and she is not my cousin, Anne. I'm sorry, Aunt, I should have broken the news to you years ago," Mr. Darcy said.

"But, but, this is not to be borne! You were destined for each other. Your uncle, my brother, he will agree with me on this! Yes, yes, I will go to

Matlock and have him force you to marry Anne!" she threatened.

Mr. Darcy stood up from his desk and walked slowly over to his aunt so that his full height towered over her. "You will do no such thing, and any claim you make about me ruining Anne, or other tricks you might conceive on the way, will fall on deaf ears. Your brother believes you are touched in the head over the whole matter, and insulted, perhaps, that you did not choose his sons for this illustrious match," he said off-handedly.

"You rogue! You fiend! All those years of trespassing on my kindness—"

"Your kindness? You are mistaken, Madam. My kindness, sorting out your estate every spring when I have more than enough property to manage in my family's portfolio."

"But, I AM your family!" she sputtered.

Mr. Darcy shook his head. "You are my mother's sister. As for love or affection to me or my sister, you have given none."

Another knock on the door alerted Darcy that his sister had come. So he lowered his voice to offer Lady Catherine a threat of his own. "Go enjoy my hospitality for you will not be welcome in this house again. You have insulted and harmed someone very dear to me for the final time. Make a fuss and upset my sister, and I will throw you out in the middle of the night without an ounce of guilt."

"You, you, you wouldn't," she charged. When Mr. Darcy pressed his lips in the firm expression of rebuke, she doubled down on her assertion. "You couldn't!"

"But I can. And I shall."

When Darcy walked over to the door and opened it for his sister, his aunt had the presence of mind, and self-preservation, to exit the study once Georgiana moved out of the way.

"Hello, Aunt—" Georgiana began, but as Lady Catherine barged past her, the greeting choked in her throat. Bewildered, she looked at her brother for an explanation for the rudeness.

"She's exhausted from her travels," he explained, retreating back to his desk to review the small list of tasks inked in his journal. Not wishing to overlook anything, he wanted all of his business completed before he left for Hertfordshire after Christmas.

"You wished to speak to me?" Georgiana asked.

"Err, yes, please close the door," he said, suddenly feeling all of the awkwardness of the entire situation. "Georgie, forgive me, I have told you a falsehood."

"Oh? But, you've instructed me to never lie. So, you," she fumbled as the confession from her brother caught her off guard, "You must have had a good reason."

Mr. Darcy sighed. "No, in fact, it was a moment ago. I am so accustomed to sparing you any sort of displeasure, that I place you at a disadvantage, as evidenced by my failings this summer."

Georgiana's lower lip quivered, as she suddenly feared her brother's need to see her. "Oh, please Fitzwilliam, I shall never do anything so stupid again. I promise! Please do not send me away with Lady Catherine!"

"Lady Catherine? Oh no," he chuckled, trying to set his sister at ease. "No, no, please, sit down and hear what I will say," he began, suddenly wishing he kept spirits other than whisky in his study. The thought of needing to keep brandy and port in his study for the comfort of women, like he had witnessed Mr. Bennet offer to his daughter, made him smile. It would not be long now until Pemberley enjoyed the better balance of a proper Master and Mistress in the home.

"Lady Catherine was rude to you just now

and I explained it away with a falsehood. In a manner much worse and far more insulting, she has harmed someone especially dear to me," he said.

"Miss Elizabeth?" she guessed, twisting her fingers gently in her lap.

Her brother nodded.

"So much so, that I am asking, nay, begging you for a monumental favor."

Georgiana gazed at her brother with curiosity, tilting her head gently to one side as she contemplated this new change in their roles. For the first time in her life, her elder brother by more than a decade needed her assistance. Enthusiastically, she used the words he often said to her:

"Anything within my power to give shall be yours."

Darcy sat stunned for a moment at the display of her maturity and instead of a young lady, he heard the words of a grown woman speaking back to him. He took a breath, and made his request, feeling that this moment would change things forever between them. He would have to treat her as a lady in her own right, as Elizabeth had spoken about in the churchyard, one who wished to have a voice in her own life.

"I would like for us to travel to Hertfordshire

for Christmas, ahead of schedule," Mr. Darcy said. "We will stay with the Bingleys at Netherfield Park."

Georgiana looked at him in surprise. "But Pemberley is our home. We always spend Christmas here." The words tumbled out before she could think about them. Since the death of their parents the one tradition Fitzwilliam had maintained for them both was Christmas together, at Pemberley. Invitations, demands, and even bribes from other family members had never moved her brother's plans.

"I worried it was too much to ask, certainly, you should not have to give up your holiday for our aunt's horrific behavior."

Georgiana nibbled on her lower lip, wishing to give her brother a more mature consideration of his request. "What did Aunt Catherine do?"

Fitzwilliam sighed. "To be honest with you I know only a small amount of the tale, from our aunt herself. However, I can imagine how terrible of a lashing that tongue of hers gave. She arrived at Longbourn unannounced and demanded that Miss Elizabeth never accept an offer of marriage from me and told her that I was engaged to her daughter."

"She really is dicked in the nob!" Georgiana's

eyes widened as she covered her mouth with her hands at her brother's reaction of shock.

"Georgiana!"

"I'm sorry, I'm sorry, Richard says that about her all the time," she confessed.

Closing his eyes, Mr. Darcy frowned, until he let out the breath he had been holding. Then he gave a small laugh, hearing his cousin's voice. He couldn't fault his sister one bit, Richard did say the phrase anytime the subject of their aunt came up.

Braving speaking again, Georgiana retracted her earlier sentiment. "This is grave, indeed. If Aunt Catherine was even half as harsh in her speech with Miss Elizabeth, then she is likely devastated over the ordeal. We must go to Hertfordshire early, and, and, and..." she struggled for what action to take that did not order her brother to propose marriage. Finally, she settled on a clever phrase that said much the same: "Cheer her for Christmas!" she suggested.

Mr. Darcy gazed at his sister with eyes glassy from emotion and weariness. Rising, he turned away from her, toward the window. It was growing dark outside, and the sky was clear; the stars began to twinkle in the early dusk only winter offered. He closed his eyes and thought back to the last time he had seen Elizabeth before he had left to spend Christmas with his sister. The pain of making the first choice between the most important women in his life was a novel concept, one he soon realized would not always go in his sister's favor.

"I must ride tomorrow morning to finish the last of the tenant business with Mr. Chapman," he said. He looked out the window again and saw that it was snowing, drifting down lightly from the clouds. The Grounds staff completed their work by lantern light, securing the tools and carts for another day. If it snowed all night, tomorrow morning the ride with his steward would be quiet and peaceful, as the first dusting of flakes always muffled the sounds of the forest.

Georgiana rose from her seat, attracting her brother's attention away from the window. "I shall pack tonight. And during our visit? I shall endeavor to behave most charmingly with Miss Elizabeth, and all of her sisters. Oh! Once you are married, I shall have the newfound joy of five sisters!" she said, giddily.

Mr. Darcy opened his mouth to caution his sister that he and Miss Elizabeth were not officially engaged to wed, but could not find the heart to disappoint his sister more. Besides, he had more than one sign that when he offered for Miss Elizabeth's hand in marriage properly, he would be made the happiest of men in the kingdom.

"I believe we can leave shortly after luncheon if I am efficient in my work."

Georgiana surprised her brother with an unexpected embrace, one so forceful, he had barely enough time to lift his arms to wrap around her.

"We won't be alone anymore, will we?" she asked, laying her head on his chest. Just as a lump formed in Mr. Darcy's throat, and his emotions threatened once more to overwhelm him, Georgianna's youthful exuberance spared them both.

She pulled back, and in a most serious tone asked a question he had not even considered: "Brother, what should you like for me to bring to Hertfordshire as gifts to my future sisters?"

CHAPTER 21

Christmas Eve at Longbourn struggled between feelings of grief and hope. The Gardiners arrived the day before from London, with Mr. Gardiner accompanying his wife, sister, and the widower Phillips to the grave of Magdalene Phillips to pay his respects. Elizabeth volunteered to stay behind with the Gardiner children and their nurse to see them properly settled into their room. In years past, the Christmas holiday was the one large reunion of the Gardiner children, as it was the only time of year Mr. Gardiner, an importer and exporter in London, could be assured of time away from his business.

It was shortly after supper that her Aunt and Uncle Gardiner imparted the good news to Lizzy that her uncle's business had taken a turn for the better. So much so, they planned a grand tour of the Lake District in the summer and invited her to attend.

"Yes, Simon is a capable lad, I taught him myself, you see? And Mr. Hobbs would never allow him to get into too much trouble," Mr. Gardiner boasted of his new head clerk and how his long-time partner in his business could provide guidance.

Elizabeth was at a loss for words as her heart twisted most painfully for many reasons. She had not yet had the chance to tell her aunt and uncle about what transpired between herself and Mr. Darcy. Additionally, even after the visit of Lady Catherine de Bourgh, not all of her family knew of the expected proposal. She felt both silly and tempting fate to be so bold as her mother and lay it all out.

"Lizzy? I should have thought you to be delighted? With Jane marrying, you cannot expect things to be as they are now between you two. A long trip to the Lake District should be a jolly adventure for a young woman to look forward to," Mrs. Gardiner advised.

Elizabeth nodded and sipped her cider, looking around the room for any rescue from her predicament. She never was one to lie convincingly, and of all people, her Aunt Gardiner would sniff out a half-truth before one regained their breath. Jane was busy entertaining Mr. Bingley with her mother in close earshot. Her father comforted Uncle Phillips with a game of backgammon, and Lydia and Kitty were nowhere to be found.

Instead, her savior came in a most unexpected form: her sister Mary.

"Since the fire, we've all learned the plans of the Almighty are not to be tested. Whereas ye know not what shall be on the morrow. For what is your life? It is even a vapor, that appeareth for a little time, and then vanisheth away," Mary said, solemnly.

The Gardiners accepted their most pious niece's explanation for Lizzy's reaction.

"Oh, my dear, how insensitive of me," Aunt Gardiner scolded herself, then reached out to touch Elizabeth's hand.

Weakly, Elizabeth offered her a smile of understanding. "It is a most generous invitation, and I should love to go if circumstances permit. Tell me," she said, willing to make a small risk of revealing her private business, "do you expect to travel through Derbyshire?"

"Derbyshire?" Uncle Gardiner repeated, with a

grin and wink to his bride. "Indeed we plan to stop in Derbyshire! Why Lambton is where your aunt grew up and we should be the worst relations in the world if we did not stop for a visit."

Mrs. Gardiner blushed as her husband lifted her hand to his lips. Elizabeth watched the exchange and sighed. She had forgotten one of the chief reasons she and her sister Jane enjoyed visiting with the Gardiners so much was their easy affection and regard for one another.

"Lambton, I remember as a little girl you telling me about the place. What other villages are close by?" Elizabeth asked.

"My home village is equal distance between Matlock and Chatsworth, but the closest village and estate is the home of the Darcy family, at Pemberley."

Elizabeth sputtered as she had tried to take a sip of cider while her aunt described the location. Recovering herself quickly, she felt relieved that she had not spilled any on her gown.

"Pemberley? As in Mr. Darcy's home?"

Lydia and Kitty burst into the parlor in extravagant gowns and pieces of wardrobe borrowed without permission from Elizabeth and Jane. Skipping around the room, they threw dried flower petals and demanded the attention of everyone in the room. Still, Aunt Gardiner and Elizabeth tried to continue their conversation.

"Yes, the same. I hear the new Mr. Darcy is a fine gentleman."

"A fine gentleman?" Elizabeth asked, unwilling to reveal she agreed with her aunt.

"Yes, from what I hear, he is a handsome and refined man."

Lydia halted in front of her aunt, her eyes wide with delight.

"Oh, Lizzy knows Mr. Darcy is handsome. Mighty fine. She's painted a miniature of him and keeps it at her bedside!" the youngest Bennet daughter exclaimed.

"Lydia!" Jane scolded and Mr. Bingley howled most ungentlemanly-like as the poor man was deep in his cups and drinking more.

"Hear, hear to Miss Elizabeth and my friend, Mr. Darcy! Where, where is the poor devil?" The very drunk Mr. Bingley looked around him as those who had also imbibed too much by this point agreed with him, and those still sober coughed with discomfort.

Jane patiently reminded Mr. Bingley that Mr. Darcy was not scheduled to arrive for another five days. Amidst the cackles of merrymaking around her, Elizabeth closed her eyes and inhaled a deep breath. Since the visit by Lady Catherine de Bourgh, her father had not received a letter from Mr. Darcy. The man had written faithfully, twice per week. And now, there was a week of nothing. She tried to believe it was a case of mismanaged post, or a messenger's horse gone lame.

"Well, he sure is missing a bloody good party!" Mr. Bingley shouted, receiving a rallying cheer from Mr. Bennet and Uncle Phillips, who had matched the gentleman in drinking.

"We are so blessed that Mr. Darcy likes Lizzy, I dare say she is not likely to capture the attention of a third gentleman," Mrs. Bennet offered.

Elizabeth reddened deeper than a shade of tomato and felt tears pricking her eyes from her embarrassment. No one contradicted Mrs. Bennet's swipe at her daughter, so Kitty took the opportunity and lull in conversation to clap her hands.

"We have prepared skits for you!" Kitty pronounced, nodding to Mary who reluctantly rose to play the piano.

The skits were bawdy and hilarious, making fun of a miserly character who had cheated the world for his purse and then when he fell on hard times, was offered no help. Between each girl and the few footmen they had enlisted to play their parts missing cues and forgetting their lines, everyone in the room had sides that ached from laughter. It became the perfect means by which Elizabeth found a way to leave and retire for the evening.

Her bedroom lay in complete disarray as it appeared when her younger sisters rummaged for their costumes, they left nothing beneath consideration. Still, the room felt empty, lonely — two emotions Elizabeth felt a particular kinship. She often retired before the rest of her family, and certainly Jane. Despite the subtle snub of the Bennet family by Mr. Bingley's sisters, who rarely came to call anymore, nothing appeared to make Mr. Bingley falter in his love for Jane. And so on evenings when he dined at Longbourn, he rarely left earlier than ten o'clock at night if he could at all help it.

Songs of joy and shouts of laughter drifted upstairs and Elizabeth dashed across the room to close the door to the sounds of a revelry she could not join. She lit a candle and hastily searched the top drawer of the small table beside her bed. She discovered the miniature of the handsome man from Derbyshire remained unmolested by her sister, merely its existence exposed.

Pulling the drawer completely out, she used her hand to reach in for the letter she kept hidden away, even from Jane.

Tracing his name at the end, she suddenly wished her father had given some of the letters that Mr. Darcy wrote, even though they contained nothing similar to the sentiments contained in his first letter.

The creaking of her door alerted Elizabeth that another had entered her room. Frantically, she tried to hide both items as she turned to see who disturbed her peace, and then relaxed when she saw that it was her Aunt Gardiner.

"Lizzy?" she asked, carefully approaching as her niece straightened her posture and set the letter and miniature on the bedside table. "Oh, Little Lizzy, you are wretched!" she sympathized and pulled the young woman nearly as tall as she was into a motherly embrace.

Sobs freely flowed as Elizabeth blubbered to her aunt bits and pieces of everything that had happened since the fire. Still, Mrs. Gardiner nodded often when she did not understand in the slightest, for fear that if she stopped Elizabeth in her tale, she would never hear the ending.

"And when he left that morning, I should have told him that I loved him."

Mrs. Gardiner clucked her tongue. "But had you not asked him the day before for time?"

"Yes, but, I did not suspect that in being separated from him my feelings would undergo such a radical transformation! He was supposed to stay and we would court each other, like Jane and Mr. Bingley."

Mrs. Gardiner pressed her lips into a thin line of disapproval. "Let's not wish that you had conducted your affairs in the order in which Jane and Mr. Bingley have," she said.

Elizabeth blinked in confusion. No one had dared to say a word about Jane's brazen behavior with Mr. Bingley. It was a shock to hear her aunt even slightly condemn their attachment.

"I let him leave, and now, what if he never comes back?" she asked, utterly distracted by her emotions for Mr. Darcy.

Mrs. Gardiner sat down on Elizabeth's bed and patted the side so her niece would join her.

"Let's begin with your speech at the church. I think the two of you showed good judgment. Your letters to me reeked of suffering for the loss of your friend and all of the pains of your recovery. You were honest that you needed time, you did not feel as you do now four weeks ago. And Mr. Darcy," she said.

"Yes?" Elizabeth sniffed, wishing to not cry any more tears.

"Lizzy, Mr. Darcy is a gentleman. He is a man who will have to answer to his own conscience in all actions. He likely struggled with fulfilling your wishes after such a request as you had made of him. Perhaps he believed his feelings would not have allowed him to remain close to you without placing undue expectations on your recuperation. I do not believe he had an easy decision. But if I had been able to advise him, I should have told him the decision to leave was wisest."

"Wisest? However so?"

Mrs. Gardiner squeezed her niece with a tight embrace, delighting in the complete absence of Elizabeth's normal logic and sense. "Poets for millennia have told us again and again," she answered.

Elizabeth scowled as her thoughts and feelings were far too jumbled for her to play guessing games.

"Absence makes the heart grow fonder."

Mrs. Gardiner gently rubbed Elizabeth's upper back and offered to undo the buttons on the back of her gown so she did not have to call a maid. Elizabeth allowed her aunt's care to soothe

the aching beast of a heart that pumped furiously in her chest.

Before her aunt was to leave her, and after she accepted her wishes for a good night's rest, Elizabeth shared the one last part that still tormented her mind.

"But Aunt, what if he never returns?" she asked in a small voice.

Mrs. Gardiner laughed at her niece's silly worry.

"My dear, you know where he lives. If he never returns, I'll take you to Pemberley myself to demand satisfaction."

CHAPTER 22

After a night of crying over circumstances she could not control, Elizabeth Bennett woke with a singular mission and her mind on Christmas morning. She would locate every distraction at her disposal to avoid pining any further from Mr. Darcy.

Unfortunately, after she dressed and went downstairs, she soon found herself to be the only person in the household awake. She found Mrs. Hill, the housekeeper, heavily fatigued as she removed a tray of dishes from the parlor.

"My family enjoy themselves late into the evening?" she asked.

Mrs. Hill chuckled softly. "Wee hours of the morning, I'm afraid. Mr. Bingley only left a few hours ago."

"Could a tray be brought to the library?" Elizabeth asked, expecting to find her father there. The housekeeper nodded and Elizabeth smiled weakly before she ran off to find a book to read.

The library offered a peaceful retreat, but a brief one, as there was no one in there to engage her mind away from thinking about Mr. Darcy. She knew all of the titles on each shelf by heart, and nothing captured her imagination as she thought ill of her family for carrying on so late into the night. Though, had she considered that being the sole member of the household to awake with the sunrise, it was she who was throwing off the natural rhythms and allowing the staff to rest.

The door opened and a young maid carried in a tray of drinking chocolate, and a few pastries left over from the evening before. Elizabeth waited until she was alone once more to nibble at the food, but found her usual appetite waning. Her heart simply could not agree to the plan of the day.

Pacing her father's study, Elizabeth began to talk to herself to mimic the exchange she might receive with her father.

"No Lizzy," she said in the deepest baritone she could muster, "what plagues you, Child? You are restless and afflicted. Ha!" she laughed, imagining her father's reaction. "You ARE crossed in love!"

Changing her voice to normal, she answered the empty desk.

"Yes, Papa, and I should like to be uncrossed! If Mr. Darcy is on his way to Hertfordshire, even should I pen him once more, it shall never get there in time."

"And if he is not on his way? If your letter you sent with your mother's blessing did not reach him?" she asked herself, again in her father's voice.

Elizabeth stood for a moment still, closing her eyes and listening for any sounds of the household stirring. She was disappointed once more as not even the Gardiner children were awake yet. She blew out a breath and tried to think through her unhelpful emotions of anxiety, dread, and fear of rejection.

"I was in the right to wait. I required time to heal, and he needed separation to know our attachment is not out of gratitude," she said, taking a breath after each reminder of the truth.

"What then?" her father's voice asked in her mind, making her believe he would be proud of her for discovering her own growth.

Elizabeth opened her eyes and her focus fell

upon the desk once more and she braved sitting in her father's chair. "It matters not if the letter will never reach him. I can write my thoughts and proceed from there," she reasoned. And as she wrote line after line, similar in a fashion to the lengthy letter he gave to her, she began to think more and more logically once she purged herself of the burden of her emotions.

As she inquired about his plans to travel to Hertfordshire, and beseeching him to come back as soon as he was able, in case he did not receive her last note or understand its meaning, she cursed herself for her foolishness. Of course, her father would not receive Mr. Darcy's travel plans, they would have been sent to Netherfield. Mr. Bingley was present the previous evening and instead of taking an opportunity to ask him, she squandered it.

"Jane!" Elizabeth realized her sister might hold the same intelligence as her beau. She had not thought to ask Jane because she believed her sister would have shared any news if she had it in her possession. Then Mr. Bingley's outburst from the previous night played in her memory.

"Hear, hear to Miss Elizabeth and my friend, Mr. Darcy! Where, where is the poor devil?" Mr. Bingley had said. Why would Mr. Bingley have thought Mr. Darcy was present unless there had been a possibility of the same? The man was drunk, but not touched in the head. There had to be some truth to his belief that Mr. Darcy was supposed to be at Longbourn on Christmas Eve.

She read over her letter once more and blushed at the amount of time spent on her heartache. Set upon a new solution of action, she abandoned her missive, crumpling the parchment and casting it into the fire.

Drumming her fingers on the desk, Elizabeth tried to wait to see if she should wake up her sister. Her burning desire to know once and for all about Mr. Darcy and his plans to return drove her to near madness.

Interrupting her dwindling self-control, the library door opened and a young footman entered with a message. He paused when it was not Mr. Bennet sitting behind the desk, but Miss Elizabeth.

"A message from Netherfield, sir, er, ma'am?" he asked, as Elizabeth stretched out her hand with authority.

As the footman hesitated, Elizabeth slanted her eyes daring the young man to question her. He shrugged and handed the note over, leaving Elizabeth alone.

Her hands shaking, she opened the message not even sealed.

Mr. Fitzwilliam Darcy and his sister, Miss Georgiana Darcy, arrived last night.

Your Humble Servant,

Mr. Nichols

Elizabeth grinned and swung her feet in giddy elation. Of course, her father had a secret mole at Netherfield Park sending him messages, how else had the man never asked for clarification when he questioned Elizabeth and Jane? The man had known more than he had ever let on!

Leaving her father's study, she ordered for Franny to be saddled immediately as she rushed above stairs to change into the proper attire for a cold morning ride.

"But Miss Lizzy, where should we say you've gone if asked?" Mrs. Hill asked.

Elizabeth paused at the banister and handed the note to the housekeeper.

"Give my father this and he will know."

CHAPTER 23

When Elizabeth arrived at Netherfield Park, a carriage waited in the drive. She pulled the reins of Franny to bring the horse to a stop as Mr. Darcy opened the door to the carriage and leapt out. He took the place of groom, before handing the reins to the footman who scrambled down from his post to help his Master.

Her cheeks reddened from the cold and wind of riding so quickly, her forest green cloak askew from where it had been carefully pinned, she cared not about her appearance. Looking down at his waiting strong hands, she beamed at him and allowed the man who had so thoroughly disturbed her peace to gently help her dismount.

"My eyes cannot believe it, you are here," he whispered.

"My father had a spy," she explained, realizing he had not released her yet. Frustrated at the slowness of her rider's dismount, Franny grew restless and stomped on the ground, shaking her neck. Two groomsmen approached as Fitzwilliam protectively shielded Elizabeth from the impatient beast. Giggling as she was ensconced against his great coat, she pushed back to speak clearly.

"If you feed her, she will settle splendidly," Elizabeth explained.

"But she needs a cool down, sir?" the groomsman asked Mr. Darcy.

Mr. Darcy looked to Elizabeth and when she shook her head, he echoed her order. "The lady knows her animal. Feed the horse and then allow her a walk in the paddock."

As Mr. Darcy began to escort Elizabeth to the steps, a voice called out from the carriage. Fitzwilliam cringed and covered his face with his gloved hands briefly. "Forgive me, I must have been distracted," he said.

"Yes, you must be," Elizabeth said, laughing as she waved warmly to the young woman calling for Fitzwilliam.

Double stepping back to the carriage, Mr. Darcy assisted his sister down, and she wasted no time with a silly escort. Laughing, she walked faster than her brother, and hurriedly curtsied before Elizabeth, the antics of the sister and brother granting Elizabeth the most comforting comedic performance.

"You must be Miss Elizabeth Bennet," she squeaked, so overcome with excitement. "I am Georgiana Darcy," she said, curtsying again.

Elizabeth nodded as Fitzwilliam hurried up behind his sister, huffing from the doubled efforts of physical exertion.

"Georgiana, you should wait for an introduction."

"Yes, Brother, I ought to wait," she said, obediently, then flashed a smile to Elizabeth and leaned in with a conspiratorial whisper, "but he didn't wait, did he?"

Elizabeth shook her head in agreement.

Exasperated to be outvoted for the first time, Mr. Darcy escorted both of the women inside and Elizabeth suddenly felt a wave of nervousness grip her heart as it was one thing to be so spun up into a need to act, that she rode directly over to Netherfield Park. It was an entirely different problem now that she was in Mr. Darcy's presence and she did not concoct a plan beyond seeing Mr. Darcy.

Leading the ladies to the first floor parlor in a desultory fashion, Mr. Darcy whispered to the butler, Mr. Nichols, for a message to be sent to Longbourn to alert the household of Miss Elizabeth's safe arrival. Elizabeth blushed as she caught Mr. Nichols' eye and was about to look away in shame, but the former valet for Mr. Bennet winked at the young woman he'd known since she was in swaddling clothes.

"Right away, sir," he agreed.

To all appearances, the manner in which the staff listened to Mr. Darcy, no one would have guessed he was not lord and master of the home.

The parlor, cast in the ghosts of white sheets for the last five Christmas seasons, stood decorated as though to make up for lost time. The heavy curtains were drawn to allow in the preciously short winter sunlight, with tallow candles burning in a dozen candelabras to match the sun's rays in warmth in the corners where the large bay windows did not reach. Someone had covered the mantle in the forest's offerings filling the room with a scent that masked the candles: a mixture of pine sap and the woodsy earthiness of evergreen branches.

Elizabeth stood arrested by the sight and welcoming smells of the room, before turning around to see Mr. Darcy staring intently at her. She unfastened her cloak and handed the outdoor garment to the maid waiting upon her. Mr. Darcy shed his great coat to reveal the fine cut of his navy blue coat.

"What a relief we did not leave for Longbourn," Georgiana announced as the servants left the room. "I shall return right away," she said, bowing out of the parlor before her brother could say a word.

Suddenly alone, Elizabeth and Mr. Darcy chuckled at each other, looking away briefly in embarrassment. Finally, he approached her, and lifting her hand, led her over to sit near the fireplace.

"Your hands are very cold," he commented.

She shrugged. "I should have worn thicker gloves."

Another silence fell as they both struggled with what to say. Elizabeth recalled her father's observation of Mr. Darcy that he was not one to fill a silence with unnecessary words. At the moment, however, she recalled many words that felt very necessary.

Suddenly, they both tried to speak at once, adding more to the morning's folly. When they both waited again, Mr. Darcy spoke first.

"Merry Christmas, Elizabeth," he offered.

Elizabeth leaned forward in her seat. "How did you know to come?"

He reached into his coat to retrieve the contents of his vest pocket. A tattered piece of ribbon and a simple piece of parchment, folded. Opening it, he cleared his throat and recited.

"No matter what your aunt says, return here and any question you might ask me, you'll have my hearty consent," he said, not daring to look up at her. Folding it and putting it away again, he held the shred of ribbon between his forefinger and thumb. "It was not signed, but my aunt did come to Pemberley with the most horrific tale of her behavior to date. And I'm sorry," he uttered, his voice cracking as he imagined the worst imaginable and finally braved looking at his beloved. "I am so sorry she ever came to abuse you," he said.

Elizabeth blanched, but watched his fingers earnestly rub the ribbon. She suddenly understood how his worry and anxiety had matched her own, taken out upon the poor token of her esteem. She forced herself to look at him and gave him an honest smile.

"It is well, now that you are here."

She reached out and placed her hand over his, holding the ribbon so fiercely. Her touch stilled his fingers, and she heard him gasp. But this was as far as she could go, she had sent the note and rode to Netherfield Park. He had to close the final gap in their understanding.

Thankfully, he understood the pleading in her eyes.

"Our separation tormented me every moment, I worried needlessly, thanks to the hope my aunt granted to me, that your regard for me, what little existed before I left, would dwindle."

"Quite the opposite! You had not quit the county but a few hours and I began to suspect I was the most foolish woman in all of England to warn you off."

"I knew enough of your disposition to be certain that, had you been absolutely, irrevocably decided against me, you would have acknowledged it to Lady Catherine, frankly and openly—"

Again, she allowed her nerves to overtake her

into an outburst of humility. "Yes, you know enough of my *frankness* to believe me capable of *that*."

He looked at her with a conflicted expression on his face. Still, setting the ribbon aside, he reached out for her hands. "I dearly love and admire your frankness, from the first night I ever met you. Everyone wears a mask to curry favor, and neither of us performs for strangers."

Elizabeth sucked in her breath at such an admission and this time, held her tongue to see what else he might say.

"But I also am enraptured by your wit, kindness, and loveliness of spirit," he added. At these accolades, she again found it difficult to accept.

"You can hardly believe me all of those things," she said.

He released her hand and tapped the side of his nose. "Your father is a most helpful correspondent. Did you not paint a likeness of your friend and her sister for her family?"

"Yes, but with *your* kindness," she said, squeezing his hand that had held onto hers. Turning the tables on him, she began to enumerate his flattering qualities. "From you, I have learned what true selfless behavior and the burden of responsibility for others looks like in a gentleman."

She gazed fiercely at him to make sure he understood the contrast she was making.

When their eyes met, each knew there was never any reason to doubt the other again. Slowly, Mr. Darcy took a knee before her.

"Please, Elizabeth Bennet, will you consent to be my wife?" he asked.

"It shall be my honor. Yes!" she exclaimed, allowing him to pull her up from her seat as he rose, and into an embrace.

Mr. Darcy leaned his head down, but did not force a kiss upon Elizabeth. He barely nodded down in her direction than he suddenly felt her lips pressed against his, and then again, and again as the two learned the rhythm of this new exchange of affection. Finally, they both laughed just as the doors to the parlor opened, with Miss Bingley and Georgiana entering.

"Mr. Darcy—" Caroline Bingley started, before halting midstep to find Miss Elizabeth Bennet in a scandalous embrace with the gentleman. Georgiana rushed forward, jostling the shocked Miss Bingley with her shoulder as she maneuvered around her, caring not for the offense to her hostess.

"Is it done? Am I to have a sister?" she eagerly asked, approaching them both as Mr. Darcy refused to relinquish the woman who agreed to be his bride after such a test of fire.

"Yes, I have secured her consent," he explained, grinning to Miss Bingley and Mr. Nichols who silently poked his head into the parlor.

Elizabeth accepted Georgiana's hug, and the woman's remonstration of her earlier words.

"Five. I shall have five sisters!" she remembered, earning a nod from the sister she knew she would love best. "Fitzwilliam," she said her brother's name in a most serious voice, "you waited awfully late to deliver your Christmas gift!"

"Yes, yes he did, but it was the best gift of all, wasn't it?" Elizabeth said, earning an imperceptible squeeze from the man that would be by her side for the rest of her days.

As they made preparations to ride to Longbourn and share the happy news, with a groom riding Franny back so Elizabeth could ride in the carriage, she couldn't wait to tell Jane her greatest hope had come true. And her sister had been entirely right, as her lips still buzzed from the exchanges she had with Fitzwilliam. Kissing was indeed a dangerous behavior, and she could not wait to do it again!

The announcement of Mr. Darcy's engagement to Elizabeth Bennet on Christmas Day of 1811 cheered all of the hearts of those closest to the couple, save for Miss Caroline Bingley. She thought to perhaps thwart Mr. Darcy's engagement with Elizabeth, as she coveted the man for herself. Thankfully, Mr. Darcy took another idea from his aunt and applied the day after Christmas for a common license from the same vicar who observed their first understanding weeks ago in his churchyard.

From the ashes of the fire that consumed so much rose the beautifully bonded Bennet sisters and their beaus, united in a double wedding that lifted the spirits of their neighbors. No one forgot their loved ones lost on the fateful night of the Assembly, but a wedding reminded all that new beginnings were yet to come. Perhaps happiest of all was Mr. Bennet, as he helped his wife into the carriage after the wedding breakfast at Netherfield Park.

"I told you those two gentlemen would do good for our girls. And you were entirely wrong, Mr. Bennet, about the dark coat," Mrs. Bennet said, waving her handkerchief one last time to her daughter, Jane, now Mrs. Bingley standing upon the top step with her husband.

"Indeed, indeed, the man suits Lizzy nicely and even spared me the trouble of a second ceremony!"

THE END

ACKNOWLEDGMENTS

Thank you to #TheJaneside on Facebook for always being there for me.

This book had a few challenges given and I will list them here to see if you can spot them all.

- a way to reference a reader's favorite song from the musical *Hamilton*
- a wayward duck
- a farm horse named after Mrs. Bennet

There were two more that influenced story elements, but were changed.

I'd also like to thank the following readers for reviewing and supporting this book when it was just chapters posting. Your reviews made all the difference.

On my site, elizabethannwest.com: Dragonflyer13, SamH., Lynette, GMA1, Joan3309, Incertus, Butterfly, JohnnyFlynnFan, MrsSP9, and Bambi.

On Fanfiction.net :

GMA1, Clara84, patgzz, Elias7, JI23, Lee3619, Wyndwhyspyr, loritahubbard, Kuwpp2, mangosmum, JohnnyFlynnFan, Happy Lizzy, gabyhyatt, netherfield2000, Shelby66, roses0002, Darklightphoenix, mencia, Deadin the freezer, nancyjeanne, RHALiz, cmwinnj, Rogue1400, ThinkAboutItBabe, liysyl, kiloton, Eng Lit Lover, Joan G. Brand, PDS1, Navani1, Rosanna K, Colleen S, Saralee, Kss, Levenez, eelarahs, Dizzy Lizzy 60, Siciliana, Gigglesnco, fanofNC, gulltranquilot, rzsnider, Vespera, Deanna27, pozemom, lhatfield2013, Jansfamily4, FPJ's Mom, ArnettinCA, Lisa Cooper, Annietenbears, Maria Teresa C, Corbert4ever, Lauramari, Happywife, Another Lizzie, WayTooEasilyObsessed, trytryagain357, jesskmemmy, RuthAnneS, Nance13, r1965rd, Artemis1813, kyLeslieWat, LoveMySofa, ChrisM0519, nanciellen, Virginia, Miss Katastrophic, Not a Lizzie Fan, mariantoinette1, lpinney, Lorigami8, Gedoena, Fire.Rose.77, biffkris, JannaKalderash, troisi, FineEyesPrettyWoman, EmlynMara, Eleoopy, advalorem, Mia, Lady Dragon Rider 01, suddenlysingle, dreamiedreamer, pemsnowy, Elissa, MK543, Motherof8, Maymerdeu, LovetoRead613, Regency 1914, and many Guests!

If I missed your name, I am so sorry. I had typed each one going through the reviews. I promise I read each and every review, and may have just missed typing your name.

ABOUT THE AUTHOR

A Jane-of-all-trades, mistress to none! Elizabeth Ann West is the author of 11 novels and 11 novellas, 21 of which are story variations of Jane Austen's *Pride & Prejudice*. Her books have won reader conference awards and hit the top 50 store bestseller lists on Amazon, Kobo, Nook and the iBooks stores multiple times.

A lover of all things geeky, Elizabeth codes websites, dabbles in graphic design, and is always looking for new technology to learn and master. A former Navy wife and mother of two, her family has lived all over the United States, currently back in her home town of Virginia Beach, VA. A graduate of Christopher Newport University, you can keep up with Elizabeth on her website where she posts stories as she writes them.

elizabethannwest.com

On Facebook, she runs a private group for her readers called The Janeside

https://www.facebook.com/groups/TheJaneside

Email Elizabeth at

writer@elizabethannwest.com

ALSO BY ELIZABETH ANN WEST

The Trouble With Horses

Very Merry Mischief

To Capture Mr. Darcy

The Whisky Wedding

If Mr. Darcy Dared (mature)

Mr. Darcy's Twelfth Night (mature)

THE MORALITIES OF MARRIAGE SERIES

By Consequence of Marriage

A Virtue of Marriage

The Blessing of Marriage

The Trappings of Marriage

The Miracle of Marriage

The Fruits of Marriage (TBA)

THE SEASONS OF SERENDIPITY SERIES

A Winter Wrong

A Spring Sentiment

A Summer Shame

An Autumn Accord

A Winter Wonder

A January for Jane (bonus novella)

From Longbourn to Pemberley (Boxed Set, Year One)

A Spring Society

A May for Mary

Shop all of Elizabeth's books by visiting her site:

www.elizabethannwest.com